Wake Up. Transcend.

By Brando Christo

Sideways-8 Edition

Copyright 2012 Brandon S Christopher

License Notes: This book is licensed for your personal enjoyment only. This work is a fiction. Real people who are mentioned are only done so out of respect for being positively influential. Thanks for your support.

Follow Brando

    Facebook: Brando Christo

    Twitter: @BrandoChristo

    Twitter: @trnscndng

    Instagram:@BrandoEstoZesto

This novel is dedicated to my loving sister
CHELSEA

~ ~ ~

CHAPTER 1NE

2050 April 9th, at age 63, I, Chelsea, was dead.

But I wasn't. Floating above the same scene of my accident, I had an out of body experience, realizing this life had come to an end – so sudden. And in some fluke accident. My body sprinkled with glass and practically smeared across the warm concrete highway lines just twenty feet ahead of the limo. Blood dampened my blond hair. The shocking sight of my mangled body was apparently only a temporary part of my existence.

Was this real? My life…I had taken care of myself. I worked out. I watched what I ate. I never had any worries about my health. It's alright. It'll be OK. They're going to fix me. Help will arrive, and they'll fix me, right?

Brandon, my 65-year-old brother, and David, our escort, were inside of the squashed limo, which had a gaping hole where my body had cannoned through the windshield. Dizzy from the crash, David stumbled around to open Brandon's door. Stunned, not a word was spoken.

Brandon stepped out of the limo and looked down the desert road in the direction of my body. My neck was twisted. Large glass bits pierced my back and triceps.

One of my legs was bent backwards with bone shard sticking through Arizona sun tanned, weathered skin.

Brandon staggered like a drunk and collapsed to his knees. "Swollen, she's…" He breathed heavily. My leg swelled from the rush of blood as it escaped my body. "No," he yelled and dropped his head. He shivered and stared. David clasped his hands behind his head, trying to read Brandon. Then he approached Brandon and put a hand on his shoulder. After a pause, Brandon spoke in a calm voice, "Did she leave?"

Surprised by the clarity in Brandon's voice, "I'm afraid so," David said trying to be supportive. "She's gone."

"No," Brandon murmured. "No, you don't know," he bellowed. "You don't know," he said again, this time hushed by his own heavy breaths. "She's dead alright!" Brandon raised his volume more. "She's dead, I know…" Teary eyed, he looked at David, "…but did she leave? Are you here, Chelsea?"

David opened his mouth to speak, but didn't know how to answer.

YES, I wanted to shout out. Answer, I tried to command myself. Nothing.

Brandon's questioning, his distraught behavior, was actually the most emotion, not to mention the most communication he'd displayed in a long time. He communicated just enough to get by, but not enough to ever leave the nest and venture into the world on his own. It was my Everest.

As odd as it seemed, I found myself somewhat relieved that Brandon was sad and curious about my death because I always wanted to know his thoughts. Normally to question Brandon is to expect no response at all, or occasionally, a delayed response.

His condition, abnormal as it was, was difficult to understand, or even define. Mom and Dad and I had Brandon examined countless times. In fact, another exam is where David was taking us before the crash. It was my final attempt, or so I told myself.

Physicians always had their theories, but none could prove that he was anything other than distracted, an extreme case of Attention Deficit Disorder.

My own theories turned out to be a befuddled journey of disappointment, my college degrees a waste, my certifications a waste, my publications a waste. If my life really had just come to an end, then all I'll have to show…Well I guess the family that I started with and the family that I started. Other than that my life was indentured as a slave to an unanswered question about a boy, whom I loved more than anything, or anyone. Sure I had faced many points of dejection. If I couldn't help, no one could help. But how could I lose faith? I will find an answer, I thought. Always on the lookout, I reached out to peers who might have an unbiased approach. Maybe I was too close.

Brandon was meant to see Dr. Daniel Durig. I had met him during a convention in Palm Springs. According to medical journals he was performing more miracles than Jesus. I didn't appreciate the vanity, but I did not object to the miracles. After speaking with him, he said he wanted to do some hypnosis with Brandon. I was willing to do almost anything. If Dr. Durig's therapy didn't work, after more than half of a century of my own explorations, the only other option seemed to be a psychiatric ward.

Looking at my dear brother, at the crash scene, I wondered what was going to happen next. Was David still going to bring Brandon to Dr. Durig? What would the police do once they arrived? I half hoped that I would wake up in a cold sweat, but I didn't care about my own well being as much as I wanted to reach out to Brandon, to let him know I was still around. Really though, I didn't know where I was. Wondering if I could transport myself back into my body, the scene started to dissolve. A feeling of contentment came over, and something was pulling.

Gracefully pulling me along like a stream, whatever it was, it was electric. I felt immersed in a tingling shiver. Rejuvenating. I didn't know where I was being pulled, nor did I feel the sense of urgency to care. I didn't have a body, and at that, no body to be burdened by. I was bodiless buzzing energy. Sensational. The satisfaction was immortal, but regardless of my comfort, I couldn't have been prepared for what happened next.

A storm suddenly arrived, an intense déjà vu moment, dreamy yet enlightening. I transcended from an already altered reality into a life back in the world, and back in time.

TRANSCENDENCE - - - - Zosimos AGED 19 - - - - 330 B.C.E.

Timing is everything I think to myself, trying to get an early start on the day.

"Zosimos wait," my father yells seeing me on my horse on top of our verdant hill already embarked on my trip. "You're always fast" he says, catching his breath. Many times he's seen me in the fields chasing after our horses, just like that messenger who scouted me. *Is he trying to lure me into one of his lecturing conversations, now? I must go.* "These games, they are political," my father warns. It seems like he is about to say more, but instead hesitates. "Have a good time," he says, shooing me off.

The journey is lengthy, but potent anticipation overwhelms my senses and carries me all the way to the outskirts of Athens' city limits. I'm lost in my thoughts until the paths become paved. Shea's trotting hoofs click against the ground. The man made road certainly smoothes the ride. Too bad I have no one except Shea to share the cityscape sight, but I wouldn't trade it for a first place ribbon in my upcoming race.

Athens impresses. The city is chiseled out of stone. White bricked bridges are married to high walls. The clustered, stone houses are as disorderly and random as the lush trees in-between. All of the structures grow upward into the hillside surrendering to the overshadowing temples. My horse and I trot into the city and pass many local Athenian people carrying jugs of water, baskets and bundles of linens. There are many people. Some of the Athenians ingrained in doorway poses of their own homes gesture with playful comments. "He's a big one," I hear, as my horse and I start hiking the hill.

When I arrive at the Acropolis, the Parthenon's mesa, an old counselor also must have assumed my size meant athlete. He approaches me and escorts me to his assistant. "You are just in time," the counselor says. Hundreds of people roam the Olympic vicinity, giving mind to artists and musicians.

The assistant walks me through the crowds to one area where official priests host public trial for the competing athletes. Each athlete is required to swear an oath to Zeus, professing dedication to the gods after training for specific events for an entire year. I lied because I hadn't prepared at all and I didn't want to be disqualified.

I'm not religious, but most Greeks are, so hopefully no one finds out my secret. To this day, all I can recall is a passing messenger saw me lifting broken plows in my family's field and must have thought I was training for sport. On occasion messengers do pass our home crossing over the stream on the way to another town.

Twice, in back-to-back weeks, while I worked in the field I saw messengers observe my activities. They must have been gathering information about our property for tax purposes. A few weeks later, I was greeted with a messenger of my own. He delivered a wonderful opportunity, an invitation to the Olympic Games.

I jumped at the fortune, but if I actually had time enough to train, I would feel as privileged as royalty. My workload is never-ending, and tiresome. I'm a simple farmer, son of a farmer and grandson of a farmer. If Alala, my beautiful wife, bless her, bears me a son, he too will farm our land. *Mmm, beautiful Alala. Keep your health while I'm gone, good woman.*

A young boy bumps into me, crashing into my train of thoughts. I've lost track of my fellow competitors. Curls formed around the boy's face, highlighting his cheekbones just as mine once did. I remember being that age, back when my waist was the size that my forearms are now.

"Sorry," the boy says, tilting his head back to peer up at me. "Are you an athlete?"

"I'm a warrior" I jokingly answer in a fake baritone voice.

Startled yet persistent, he says, "I'll take your horse." I don't like leaving Shea. Then again, I remember working from a young age.

"I'm good with animals," he insists.

I look the boy in the eyes. "I'd be honored to bestow this responsibility on you," I say.

He takes Shea by the rope and leads her away through the crowds.

I hustle through the grounds and find the athletes' quarters located under the stands, harboring athletes and trainers and referees. The quarters are sectioned off in parts, separating areas for eating, and stretching and resting. The men from my event are feasting, loading up on fuel before we race. I'm too nervous to eat. However, my mouth is as dry as twine. Looking around the expansive warren, I soak up the environment like a sponge. At the same time, I reach into my shoulder pack for a stick of cane. For me, the sweet taste has always been addicting. Alala doesn't understand why I don't tire of it, especially after harvesting it all day. I chew incessantly and think about my new surroundings.

I must be the only newcomer here because the other athletes seem like they are in casual routine. A group of five spar in the corner practicing wrestling maneuvers. I know many of the athletes are signed up for multiple events, but not me. I'm just doing one race. Then I will enjoy other games and amenities as a happy fan and then head home. My mouth salivates from the cane and I drool onto my foot. *I hope no one saw that. Oh Zos, enjoy this time.* I slide my gear on, trying to distract myself from my nerves. Pretty soon we'll be out there in the field of competition so I need to focus.

"The Warrior 400," the referee announces as six of us, wearing body armor and carrying shields, march onto the track in front of more people than I have ever seen gathered together in my whole life. The marching men around me, whom I'm far too inferior an athlete to call equals, confidently wave at the cheering crowds. This is kind of a late thought, but I'm wondering if these other athletes have a special technique to run this race. I just know I'm supposed to wear my gear, carry my shield, and run as fast as I can. Hopefully I don't embarrass myself. *Oh well, no expectations. Just run.* Moments of the day speed by as it is. If I don't pay attention, I'll miss the race. I look to the fans again who have doubled in size. Where did they come from? I never imagined so many people would be here.

The referee informs the crowd of our names, cities and that the winner of this race proves to be the fiercest warrior prepared to fight for Greece. I know it's for show, but what a humbling statement. I'm excited enough, almost breathless, my emotions taut, my muscles twitching like those of an anxious race horse at the starting gate. We line up. It will be a short, yet grueling 400 strides in length.

At the sounding crack of a whip, the race begins. We explode off the line. Shields and armor clang together. Our powerful legs propel our bodies, while our arms pump back and forth edging our momentum on trying to gain extra crawls over each other. After ten or twelve running motions like this, I unexpectedly find myself alone, moving with the grace and speed of a cheetah chasing his prey. No more competitors. No more fans. The shield I'm carrying is buoyantly light. My energy intensifies. All I can see is the dirt immediately in front of me. Sprint. Sprint. Sprint. Reality returns and I cross the finish line strides ahead of my competitors. The crowd hails my victory and after a momentary delay I realize I won the race. I must have set a record. The unbridled euphoria of the moment raises my spirits more than ever before.

"That was some race for an untrained athlete, farmer," I hear a sleazy voice say whilst I rest back in the athletes' quarters.

"Oh no," I think to myself.

"I am General Phillip," he proclaims before I can respond. It's obvious he's some sort of commanding officer because he is accompanied by half a dozen guards. I start to stand from my chair, but he motions for me to stay seated.

"I didn't –" before I begin, the general interrupts me.

"Don't worry. You are here because of my good graces," General Philip says trying to transform an engraved scowl into something a little more pleasant. "One of my messengers said you would be good and he was correct. You really inspired our people with that performance."

It must have been the sugar, I thought, waiting to see what he wanted. Apart from the fact that the athletic quarters have filled up with scribes and who knows who since my race, I'm surprised I missed the general's entrance because his presence is intimidating. It must be because he's so small, not just compared to me, but even his guards.

"I'm not an athlete," I stammer.

"Don't be foolish," General Phillip says. "You are a true athlete - A warrior."

"Thanks," I reply bashfully.

"Our people now want to praise you as a servant to Greece and as one to the gods," he says. I look down reminding myself that I'm not a man of faith. "More public displays like that and you might consider yourself one of the gods. You are already the size of a god." I find myself trying not to laugh at how small he is. "We could use a performance like that on the battle field."

Ok I see. It was just a race, I think to myself. He came on strong with more pressure saying, "You are a Greek citizen no doubt."

"Yes," I answer, "but I have a family waiting."

"Most of my men have families waiting," the general says. "An athlete, a warrior like you is sure to return home safely, and with glory. General Philip says so." Insisting he adds, "It's settled." "I declare it your obligatory duty for Greece," he proclaims and storms off, escorted by his guards.

My stomach rises to my throat. I'm unable to swallow the reality of what just happened. *What a mistake. Why did I need to compete in the games of the Olympiad? It hasn't been for the art, not the poetry.* Before I commiserate too much, a truly enchanting voice calls out, "General Philip," intriguing everyone in the room and catching the general before he exits. "May I have a word?"

This grey-bearded man is a man to be noticed. He's not an artist. He's not a politician. He's garbed like an academic. *He could be a scholar. Could that be Aristotle – the all-knowing man? Obviously he'd be at the games, but could that be him?*

Like the rest of the room I pretend to mind my own business. Many of the other athletes do mind their own business. I can't. I've got nothing else to do except worry about my fate and my family. Is this man talking on my behalf, I ask myself doubtfully?

After he and the general finish talking, the general leaves with his guards. This new man of the moment approaches me.

"Zosimos, right?"

I stand from of my chair.

"I'm Aristotle."

It is him. He's a pous or two taller than the general - almost my height.

"Please have a seat," he says. "In fact, I shall sit too."

As he turns and reaches for a chair I compare his beard to my memory of father's. *Same thickness, but Aristotle's is better groomed.* No, that's not it, I determine, trying to discover what makes this man appear so stoic.

He slides his chair close to mine.

"You know me," I say.

"Well of course," he says. "I'm charting all of the results from the games so participants can be honored in the future." He looks around, acting aloof. "Your family harvests sugar cane?" he says, changing topics.

"Yes," I say, wondering how he can tune into all of his surroundings and continue to be conscientious with me.

"What stream provides irrigation for your family's farm?"

"Olynthiakos," I answer, recalling the stream's width. Now that I've been away from the water source that I've spent my entire life near, it's bizarre to have to imagine it, but I can do so as if I'm looking from my house. It's far off, past our stables and past our field to the shoreline, but I can see the rippling stream clearly.

"And does the Olynthiakos stream have any supernatural mineral that helps you grow sugar cane that I could not reproduce in my own gardens?" Aristotle asks, interrupting my imagination.

"No," I say, caught by surprise. "There is no supernatural mineral."

"Do you have some?"

Unintentionally, I pause for a second. "Yes, absolutely," I say as I search for my pack to get a couple sticks of cane. We both indulge in the cane's sweetness.

"Wonderful timing," he says. "Right away one can judge the sharp, sweet taste and then an amusing texture for the tongue followed by a second burst of sweetness," Aristotle says. "It's very good."

We both stare off into the abyss, enjoying the sugar until a droplet of drool dribbles into Aristotle's beard. He's enjoying the sugar cane so much that he doesn't seem to care.

He stirs our silence with a statement similar to the general's. "It's settled then," he pronounces. "You can work for me at The Academy, and in the gardens there. If you design for me a sugar cane patch, you will not have any military duty. And you can return home as soon as you are done. You have a family waiting your return I presume. I will even allow you time to study, if you're interested. You will be home before the new harvesting season. Are you interested in the life of a scholar?"

Astonished, I answer as fast as possible, "Yea," I blurt out. The sugar must have got to me again, I think as I see him chuckling. "Perfect," he declares. "I'll send message to your family."

Two full moons pass during the time that I learn tenfold from Aristotle in contrast to what I share with him of my knowledge about the sugar cane crop.

We succeed in starting a patch so he will have an infinite supply. We spend moments sitting under the stars, chewing on sugar cane and discussing the meaning of life. We make time for everything. He welcomes me to join his students in his lessons about science and philosophy and ethics. I never knew how much I didn't know. I even find time to practice running. Strangely, I never seem to be as fast as I was during my gold medal race, not even after loads of sugar.

On my trek back home, back to my family, I feel like a new man. The experience at the academy, being surrounded by scholars, has surely changed my approach to how I will raise my son. Aristotle said our boy is welcome to attend the academy as a fulltime student. *Maybe the gods are watching over me after all.*

Leaving the city limits of Athens, I hear a commotion behind me. I turn my head to see General Phillip and his soldiers on horseback. His demanding demeanor solidifies that same engraved scowl. He steps off his chariot and walks up to me so I dismount from Shea.

"Are you blocking my path because you want to be a warrior?" he snarls.

I wasn't blocking his path.

"I'm returning home."

"As expected, farmer," he sinisterly says. "That's really too bad. Men, seize him," he orders.

The soldiers dismount and approach me. *Should I fight? There are too many of them.* I step back towards Shea as they draw their swords and surround me. Then I remember one of the many things Aristotle said to me at the academy. "Character is the strongest form of persuasion."

The swing of a sword comes at me and all of a sudden I see things like I'm living my last moment on earth. Instinctively I put my right hand out and grab a soldier's wrist, preventing the first sword from striking me. I see other swords on their way, but I'm seeing things so well that the soldiers and their swords seem to move at a slower pace. Again, without thought, I quickly put my left hand on the soldier's wrist. Then I use my size to my advantage by putting leverage into my legs and twirling the soldier off the ground and into the other soldiers, knocking them down.

The euphoric feeling, like when I won the race, returns. Triumph, I think to myself and head for Shea. Then what I hear, but don't see is General Philip charging from behind. Before I can find the angry, little man, he kicks my legs out from under me. Shea spooks and rears onto her hind legs. Hearing her commotion, I roll over to see her right hoof about to stomp my head.

~ ~ ~

CHAPTER 2WO

I was yet again this shivering electricity, seemingly unattached to the human world. I'd call myself the artist, or better, the spirit formerly known as Chelsea.

Waffling back and forth, was this new existence a good thing? It felt good, like a micro-massage, but so would it to wake up in a cold sweat. Imagine what I'd do. Fill my lungs with a deep inhale of oxygen. I'd wipe the sweat off my cheeks with my hands. Grab the tall glass of water that rests on the nightstand. Come to my senses. Then I'd nudge Chris and tell him about this intricate nightmare I just had. He'd listen. I'd go to Brando. I'd tell him about the dream too. He might not listen, but that would be fine. How I missed them already.

No cold sweat to appease me.

I went beyond the end of my life as Chelsea to an out-of-body experience to a sudden déjà vu storm of an in-body experience of Zosimos to back here. Who's Zosimos? Why was it so familiar to be him? Nowhere near the verge of wisdom, I was first doomed to a moment of hesitation; was this rollercoaster ride angelic or hallucinogenic?

Riddled with more questions, I wondered about reincarnation. I imagined myself starting out life in 330 B.C. swapping bodies over time until I wound up as Chelsea, to finally perish in 2050 A.D.

Now, where am I? Did one of my former lives just flash before my eyes? Was I about to go into another life?

No clarity came, just the electric current.

In fact, there was something about the electric current. Gradual. Gravitational. And it varied. I wanted to pinpoint it, but I couldn't.

It was different as Zosimos. It was there, but different.

A clear presence of vibrant electricity. I could theorize that something must have the batteries charged in order for forms of life to keep having life. That wasn't new. To really feel the energy was new. At least it seemed that way.

I observed more. Maybe I wasn't being pulled. Maybe orbiting. Maybe I orbited around some mass or the entrance to something massive.

Unsure how useful my science skills would prove to be, I was at least reassured by the fact that I was increasingly more comfortable.

Regardless, I scratched curiosity's itch. Reincarnation was a subject in which I had little if any knowledge. One of the only reasons I considered it a possibility is because it's what Dr. Durig had in mind for his hypnosis work with Brandon. Brandon could have somehow been permanently hypnotized, stuck in the visions of past lives, and needed to be un-hypnotized. Although I was now comfortable where I was, I felt it was me who needed to be *un-hypnotized*. At that moment, I would've appreciated a seat on Dr. Durig's couch, but instead, with nowhere to go and nothing else to do, I thought about Brandon.

By his teenage years, his level of coherency had nearly vanished. I thought about how various physicians always had different diagnoses; bipolar, schizophrenia, attention deficit disorder, dysfunctional personality disorder. The list went on and some of the theories were preposterous, like dream catching. It was hard to imagine anything of the sort, but we were all clueless.

Brandon would do creepy things – the type of things that would give such a strong shiver, it would make this electric current seem placid. Sometimes Brandon would walk past a TV and perfectly mimic what was happening as it was happening. A debut episode of a sitcom could be playing, and Brandon would randomly walk past and recite the same dialogue as the actor, in unison, matching accent for accent, facial expression for facial expression. Doctors had no explanation.

Sometimes he'd mutter things about places he'd never been or people with whom he had no apparent relations. During my human life, I was gravely concerned about poor Brando, about what he thought. Again, he was on my mind more than anything else.

At that point, I felt those same emotions stirring. They were rising. The electric buzzing seemed to release me as indescribable, vigorous activity manifested itself around me. Power and energy started to draw into me like electricity into a light bulb. Physical matter. Illuminated vision. I was bodied again…

TRANSCENDENCE - - - - Laurie AGED 29 - - - - 1985

Having a sign pester you day after day is unsettling at best. This tiny, obscure board posted by the side of the road is growing as big as my pregnant tummy and it will not leave me alone. I first noticed it when I learned that I was going to have a baby. Unavoidable, I pass it during drives to the grocery store. When the sign is out of sight, the words stay with me: ATONEMENT LUTHERAN CHURCH. Wouldn't you know it; it's a double sided sign so I see it on my way back home from the grocery store too. The sign also advertises the single 9:30 a.m. Sunday service. I see it everywhere I go. It started out no bigger than three by five feet, but now as I'm nearing the end of my pregnancy the sign is as large as the city of Cleveland, and not only that, it's letters are beginning to flash as though made of neon.

It has been awhile since I've seen the inside of any church. Awhile? Who am I kidding? I had given up attending church since I married Dan. That was five years ago. Even during excursions to the bank, I feel the sign forcing my pupils to dilate, attracting my attention like positively-charged magnets. The hunger gnawing away at my insides isn't just indigestion that frequently comes with pregnancy. This is something that can't be assuaged by downing a couple of Pepcid AC tablets. The sign pops up at me like a baby's pop-up book when I drive to the Y for my swimming classes. I'll be just fine once the baby arrives.

But where does the time go? 1985 - The swell of my belly is gone, replaced by this breathtaking infant. Despite the absolute rush that accompanies the first moment when I lay eyes on my new baby, despite the full knowledge that nobody else in the world since the dawning of time has ever delivered a child as gorgeous as mine, I can't settle my spirit.

The words on that roadside sign haunt me for months. I bury myself in the joys of motherhood - the 3 a.m. feedings, the 5 a.m. feedings, the 7 a.m. feedings - my, but he's hungry! Changing diapers, washing clothes, folding clothes, and not even bothering to put them in the drawer anymore become routine. Wholeheartedly, I throw myself into this new life. But I am not just fine. The hunger still gnaws at me. Finally, when Brandon is three months old, I am powerless against the unnamed, untamable force badgering my spirit.

I surrender on the next Sunday, as I mercilessly squeeze my postpartum belly into control-topped panty hose and struggle into my pre-pregnancy white linen pencil skirt with a complimenting green silk blouse. Brandon and I get ready for church. To perfectly accessorize this ensemble, I add the quilted diaper bag patterned with bright yellow ducks, scoop up downy headed Brandon and breathlessly totter to the car in heels. These heels easily navigated stairs before my pregnant belly arrived and left, leaving Brandon to stay. Now I totter to the car successfully albeit unsteadily. I stuff him into the new car seat as he spits up formula onto my blouse. "Uh", I say. Already late and not taking additional time to see if the mess will be noticeable, I briefly swab it with a cloth diaper and finish buckling Brandon into his seat, shut the BMW door and put myself behind the wheel to cautiously venture out of our gated condo parking lot and off to the small, brown building east of that annoying road sign. Contemporary, the wooden building is a style typical of Scandinavian Lutherans. An empty, wooden cross planted a few paces in front of the door quickly reveals the church's identity.

If I look devout as I warily enter the intimate sanctuary, it is because I am praying. I am praying the formula Brandon spat up on my blouse won't be obvious. The pews are positioned so that I can easily head for a seat in one of the rows just by continuing my current direction. The layout requires curious attendees to turn his or her head completely to the left to witness, maybe judge, my tardiness. There are a few who do. Bravely, I hoist up my infant for a more secure hold, the diaper bag, and what is left of my courage. Then I look around for a safe place to sit, preferably an open spot here, toward the back, so I can make a quick escape during the last hymn.

God must have a great sense of humor. No sooner do I firmly plant that sensible plan in my mind, sitting in the front pew, an older yet elegant, well groomed lady also turns around to look at me. Glow from the stained glass behind the pulpit highlights her full-bodied, blond hair. Bangs dangle in front of her forehead, but the rest is pulled up, swept away from her rosy face. She smiles and beckons me to sit beside her and her husband, Sharon and Julius. I'll politely say goodbye and make a fast escape after the last hymn. God's humor prevails. When the service is finished, Sharon not only knows every member of that church, but insists on introducing me to every last one of them. Sharon's friends went out of their way to welcome me.

When Brandon and I leave and drive out of Atonement's parking lot headed back home, I glance at the everlasting sign through my rear view mirror. Barely noticeable now, I smile feeling like I have done my duty and triumphed. I found freedom. The temptation immediately overtakes me to go back to my old ways of lazily enjoying the Sunday paper over a fresh cup of coffee. Next Sunday will be relaxing.

No sooner do I walk through the front door of our condominium than the phone rings. It's Sharon. She invites Brandon and me to return the following week. At that very moment, I know in my heart if I don't return, the sign will grow back into a monstrous torment. I acquiesce and fully commit, attending church regularly from that point on. "We shall see you then," I tell Sharon before putting the receiver back on its dock. Suddenly, I picture God smiling and telling me gently, "You cannot escape me. Jonah couldn't and you won't either." What a sense of humor.

Although that nice lady, Sharon, made me stand through all those introductions during my first visit, I've begun to get better acquainted and more comfortable with her and Julius and her many friends. Every week I show up and just as she had during our first visit there, Sharon takes Brandon into her lap and holds him the entire service. We began a new tradition of following the worship services, with fellowship with other members and casual conversation with each other.

After service on the third consecutive Sunday Sharon and Julius ask me when Brandon was born. "He arrived at Emanuel hospital on April 9th," I tell them. Sharon and Julius draw in their breath sharply and exchange meaningful gazes at each other over my head. I don't ask.

Not until several more Sundays later, when I nearly forgot Sharon and Julius had been taken aback, they explain their odd, slightly spooky behavior. Their own grandson had been born with many health complications; in and out of the hospital for most of his very short life. He died on the same day, April 9th when Brandon was born.

TRANSCENDENCE - - - - Chelsea Aged 7 - - - - 1994

"When puppies get up in the morning they always say 'Good day arf, arf'," Mom cheerily sings to Humphrey, our fluffy puppy. It is another morning, so I climb out of bed to race to mom's room.

Brandon is already awake and he is there singing along too. Humphrey sees me and wiggles and dances, and I feel just as excited. I jump onto the king-size bed adding to the pajama party. I nudge Brandon over and nestle into a comfy spot so we can all watch Dad on TV. It's the only TV we watch - Dad on the news, or Trailblazers basketball games. Otherwise we have other things to do. That's what Mom says.

"Very true Cathy," Dad says. "Do we see an end in sight to the damage?" Dad asks a lot of questions, that way he has the best information. The news is all about information. People need to know current events and the weather and the traffic. It helps with daily life. I focus on the screen again when the news goes to a commercial. Just then I feel the bed shaking.

It's Brandon shaking with his mouth halfway open, looking up to the ceiling. Mom looks panicked. Humphrey, in his frightened Maltese way, scurries into my lap. "Brandon," Mom says. "Brandon!" He is still trembling. She grips his shoulders to hold him still. "Aristotle," Brandon whispers as spit-bubbles form around his lips. *What's 'Air Toddle'?* A second later he stops shaking as he looks at his legs and then at Mom.

Mom relieved, leans over and hugs him really tight. Humphrey leaves my lap to go give Brandon puppy kisses, but Brandon still seems dazed.

"Um are you OK Brandon?" I ask.

Mom's next move - she grabs the phone and calls the station and leaves a message for Dad. "I think Brandon just had a seizure," she says in a scared voice. Then she hangs up and calls the hospital.

Dad came back on the news, but I still stare wide-eyed at Brandon.

"I'm fine," Brandon says. "What's a seizure? Is that a daydream?"

~ ~ ~

CHAPTER 3HREE

Through transcendence, there's energy. Pulled along at a lazy rate, there was actually nothing lazy about the consistent energy.

My energy was a hand tilting a glass of water into the ocean…

…and also the BB sized bubbles that rise just after inclusion…

…another wave channeling through the bubbling…

…the transient water left to explore…

…new to the flow…

…and, old to the flow.

I was invited back in it. Orbital pull. Afterlife. In-between State.

I recovered from back to back into-body experiences, one as Mom during the delivery of Brandon. The other was me, or rather, Chelsea as a little girl, who used to be me, witnessing Brandon's seizure.

The last one teased me. I was myself again. For a moment. Sure it was as a young girl, but at least I was me.

Truly, I'm not sure which experience was more peculiar: Being bodied again. Or being young again.

If only it lasted. *I'd* live it again. If I could keep my wisdom, I'd have a head start. Even if I couldn't keep my wisdom. Grand scheme, it would be worthwhile just to find Brandon and hug him tight.

Grand scheme, I didn't know the grand scheme of things.

Energy wise, each in-body experience jaunted with different feels.

And again, here in this in-between state, it's different too, much stronger than in-body. Here, I was always buzzing, and always changing. I was a morphing cloud of energy inside an energy field which seemed to expand in all directions. And there was still this core source of power that had become more prevalent.

In addition to feeling good, this electric buzz fascinated the scientist that once was a part of me. And then I remembered that this scientist, in a moment of distraction from my regular research, had come across a term that might fit the mold here – Aura. Back in the world, I would have eventually dismissed this as hipster jargon, but again here, it seemed to fit. "It's as though every aura is a different energy field; and as though every individual had a different aura; and yet there was also this endless aura," I tried to hypothesize.

I wondered if I should be called Chelsea's aura, which here would be like comparing a glass of water to an ocean. Although what confused me was that I had evidently become several different auras in a rapid fire fashion as I transcended back to Earth over and over again. I didn't know. Trying to explain this to myself was like trying to explain quantum physics to a third grader. This resulted in a typical feeling for what I knew all too well as Chelsea; the inability to define, empathize, understand. Oh joy.

What I did know was much about Brandon's seizure. I also found myself astonished that I'd forgotten about Brandon's muttering. Instantly, I figured, "Brandon must have connected to Zosimos too."

From the point in time when Brandon had that first seizure, and whispered the name Aristotle through bubbles and spit, is when I, as a little girl, and a concerned sister, started a life long journey playing detective. I was more than obsessive. Mom and Dad probably felt like they lost both kids to Brando's condition.

During my human life as a child, I started with Greek mythology, and then went on to explore the ins and outs of seizures. A seizure is when an electrical current in the brain over-fires, something I grasped at an early age.

Thinking about this from the afterlife, I wondered if Brandon had connected to the aura of Zosimos during the moment of his seizure. This possibility was insightful. What I experienced next was another occurrence of transcendence, this time my father. The orbital pull weakened as the connection to dad's aura strengthened within me.

TRANSCENDENCE - - - - Dan aged 48 - - - - 1994

With dinner over, I head to the bedroom, and into the vanity to perform my nightly ritual: Get ready for the next day's work. Suit and tie.

The infernal phone might ring in the middle of the night, calling me away on some breaking news story. I need socks too. There's no telling what color socks I'll grab if I wait to pick them out when I'm still in a sleepy, predawn stupor. I scan the suits in my closet. Ah, this one is perfect because I haven't worn it in a while. I pluck it out and hang it on a separate hook. OK, which tie works with that shirt? The blue will do.

I step in line with the vanity mirror above the sink and hold the tie up in front of my neck, thinking about the double Windsor I'll be swooping in the morning.

"I'm tired of neckties," I exhale.

It's been a long day. This outfit is good enough. The blue tie reminds me of the blue in Brandon and Chelsea's eyes, beautiful blue, sincere blue, gentle blue. Tonight is bound to be an uneasy rest because I haven't stopped worrying about Brandon since Laurie's phone call. He's so young, strong, but vulnerable. The fact is Brandon's problem makes me feel more vulnerable than ever. If only I could wave my hand and make this trauma go away, but a dad can only do so much.

Laurie said the pediatrician thinks my precious son suffers from childhood epilepsy. We are taking him in for an EEG test in a couple of days to find out. He will have to stay up the night before so he will fall asleep in the hospital. That way they can monitor his brain waves during his slumber. All this means another sleepless night ahead. But that is not important. I just need Brandon healthy. I feel such worry, such strain, and such fear. No father can ever be prepared for something like this.

In the midst of my worrying and hustling around, getting ready for the sack, I catch a glimpse of myself, and realize I'm a little rumpled. Not much to look at. Normally I'm comfortable at the sight of my rumpled reflection, because for another day, I had been the person who learned, helped and worked. I normally had reason to be proud of the person in the mirror. How unsettling it would be to see someone in that mirror who didn't deserve respect. I normally work hard just to make sure that would never happen, but sometimes that's not enough. What about the uncontrollable factors, like Brandon's condition? "Just do all you can," I say out loud almost giving up - damn it - enough speculation.

On my pillow that night, as I'm drifting into the netherworld, I find slumber, but a strange, almost giddy feeling sets in. "I'm finally in charge of my own destiny," I say as I dream about the time I lived in Chicago. I was 25, and it was the first time no one was there telling me what to do. Grade school through college was structured and someone was always there, directing my next move. The Army also dictated where I had to be, what I needed to do, and even what I was supposed to eat. Now I have the job of charting my own course, doing what I want, living where I want. Sure I have responsibilities, but I could always quit, if I so choose.

I start to dream about my responsibilities while working for Chicago-based WGN Television-Radio. I'm outside the building, but it's locked. An editor, who looks like the Marlboro man, suddenly appears outside of the building on the city's north side, and says "Don't worry man". I can see his breath in the cold air. "I've got the key," he says as he unlocks the door, lets me in and then disappears as quickly as he appeared. "Thanks buddy," I think to myself.

As I enter the lobby, the annoying, pig-tailed receptionist is behind the reception desk. She's smacking her lips, chewing on too much bubble gum and she gives me a funny look. She's too young and too inexperienced to be the first representative of this company that a visitor sees.

"Why are you so awkward?" I shout like a mad surgeon trying to remove her inner thoughts.

She gives an idiotic reply, a blank stare and more bubble gum smacks. Then the shine on my shoes catches my eye as I feel my shoes lift off the lobby floor. I'm floating! I'm levitating! That's why she... "You're excused," I tell her. She ignores my dismissal as she puts on green sunglasses and starts to blow an enormous bubble gum bubble. It *grows* like a balloon. It's going to be the size of her face in a second. Instead of waiting to see her bubble pop, my feet swing back behind me. My stomach hovers a yard off of the lobby floor. My blue tie hangs. "Forget this," I say.

I will myself to float head first into the elevator which will lift me twenty floors to the newsroom. The doors close off an elevator that logically serves as a recreational zero gravity room. Like an astronaut, I pull 360's, flip backwards, push off of the walls, and just float around.

Work aint so bad. Then gravity arrives. Quick fall towards the russet marble floor. Just before I splat like putty I find myself in my near-north side studio-apartment, a little disoriented. Anxious – Am I late for something? Deadlines. I can't be late for work.

I guessed that I'd been sleeping. Oh God, what time is it? I stumble from bed to see the clock mounted on the wall of my kitchenette. It's the efficiency kitchen. I look at the clock. The long hand is pointing directly at the twelve. The shorter hand is on the four. It's four! My shift is 3:30 to noon. I'm late!

In the chill of Chicago winters, 4 a.m. and 4 p.m. have a way of looking the same - dusky, undefined.

Am I late? Which is it, 4 a.m. or 4 p.m.? It's still dark. I need to switch back to military time.

I just stand.

Take action damn it! If I'm not there with a script –

Returning to my 48 year old body, I wake. Laurie's warmth on the right and Humphrey's warmth near my right foot. I roll to the left, to get blinded by the glaring red, digits on the alarm clock.

Adjust.

1:12 AM.

"I'm the one who needs an EEG test," I whisper. "That accelerated the heart."

I toss the sheet and blanket aside and motion to the dog that I'm going to the kitchen in case he wants to go out. Not a chance, as it turns out. As I stand next to my bed, Humphrey lowers his head and rolls his eyes as if to say "I'd join you, dad, if I wasn't so comfortable." Laurie looks cozy, curled into her pillow. I wonder if she's dreaming up any crazy nonsense like I did.

TRANSCENDENCE - - - - Laurie AGED 38 - - - - 1994

Dreaming – The script that I'm running through the teleprompter is crinkling on the right edge. I'll just adjust it. It's a little bit forward. I'll just reverse it. All I have to do is press this button. Holy crap, that's the wrong one.

The script fast forwards instead of rewinds. It's caught on a sprocket. What should I do? Oh no, it tears in half. It's destroyed and they still try to read it. I desperately grasp at each shred of the paper with my fingernails. It does no good. This is my fault.

These poor anchors, they watch in bemused horror trying to read and maintain professional composure. How will I survive this news cast? I sheepishly watch as they pick notes up off the anchor desk and finish the show.

Afterwards I go to the newsroom hoping to make a quick escape out the door to my car and never return. This internship was obviously a bad idea. To my chagrin, Dan Christopher, the main anchor, walks into the news room right behind me. I look around anxiously because I feel I need a place to hide. He is so serious. He's handsome though. Expecting that he'll be fuming, I do a double-take when I see him smiling.

He laughs. "Who taught you how to put the script together for the teleprompter?"

"I think it was Charles."

He rolls his eyes, grinning widely. "Oh I should have known."

Relieved, I smile - my classic great grandmother's half upturned smile. *That'll get him.*

He grabs a discarded script to show me how to prepare it properly for the teleprompter. "If you ever do that again, I will unscrew the nose from your face," he jokes.

~ ~ ~

CHAPTER 4OUR

I feel like I've just emerged from Plato's Allegory of the Caves: "I thought I was my shadow, but now I see."

No longer chained inside of a body. No longer imprisoned to my humanly queries.

Like a wakeup call to the dreamer, I realized that I had been Chelsea's aura all along. The in-body experiences were beautiful dreams. The out of body experiences had the epiphany feel. I was open. Vulnerable. Elightened. Epiphany. Epiphany. Or at least, that's how it felt.

In the recent "dream" episodes I had a flash from the past of mom and dad having a flash from the past.

But I noticed a major difference between being within someone's dreams compared to being within someone's aura. It was familiar because some of my studies as Chelsea were dedicated to understanding dreams, as if there I might find the answer for Brandon's condition.

I learned about REM sleep. Short for Rapid Eye Movement, it's typically the sleep with the most vivid dreams, and often occurs when a person is stressed.

In early adulthood I attempted to finish the requirements for PhD credentials by writing a thesis entitled Narcoleptic Dreams. I wanted to prove that on occasion, REM sleep was an unfair, torturous aspect of the human condition. A spooky haunting by the subconscious, I thought.

My professors gave me the opportunity for a rewrite, arguing that REM sleep is a physiological healing process.

Ironically, there were many vivid dreams during the nights following. It was another failed attempt at figuring out Brando. Sherlock was stumped, and stressed!

With Brandon, I was running through mud. It was a slow, tedious process. And I was just stubborn enough to be repeatedly egged on with a sliver of hope in what was always the next pursuit. My brain racked. I obviously went to my grave never finding…Whatever disturbed Brando…

Thinking of all this from the afterlife, as a supposed aura, I questioned my identity, and location, again.

Heaven's Spa, I lightheartedly told myself, that's where. After building up a lifetime of stress, I thought, just maybe I was self-healing through numerous visions and a kind of buzzing massage.

In reality, there was maybe a shred of truth to that.

I didn't think this is what mom meant when she described her version of heaven to the kids. During my life as Chelsea, I was more of a scientist than a preacher, but I still believed in God.

However, St. Peter was nowhere in sight. Instead I transcended into myself as a little girl.

TRANSCENDENCE - - - - - Chelsea AGED 9 - - - - 1996

Sometimes my hair can be a rat's nest. That's what Mom says.

"Yes Mom, coming." She's ready for me, to help me with my hair. I close the book and saunter past Dad and Brandon who are busy fixing their tuxedos. Dad helps Brandon with his cummerbund.

"Sweetie, I asked you to brush your hair."

"But I was reading, Mom." She frowns, not happy with my answer.

"Tonight is the ship's first formal night. We're sitting at the captain's table and your hair looks like a rat's nest."

"I'm sorry. At least, I'm wearing a dress."

"Here, sit," Mom says as she starts to brush out the knots.

"Ouch."

"Oh hush. OK, now I will show you how to curl, but you need to take charge." She uses that statement a lot - 'take charge'. She wants me to 'take charge' of myself, be independent.

The idea makes me think of Brandon, as I always do. I look at him, his hair, perfectly combed into the same anchorman style that Dad wears. It's been combed that way so many times, I don't think it will ever be messy. He stares into the mirror, but not at himself. *I wonder what he's thinking.*

Dad puts cufflinks into the button holes of Brandon's French cuff sleeves.

"What was your favorite part of Costa Rica today?" Mom asks. She must know I'm in a bad mood. *I don't feel like playing this game.*

"Not doing homework."

"That's not why we travel. And you can finish your homework tomorrow. Come on, you'll have to do better than that. Try again. Didn't you like the rain forest?"

"I liked the monkeys in the trees." *She can meet me halfway with that answer.*

She smirks.

"Mom, I'm worried about Brandon," I whisper. "Do you think he'll get better?"

"You know what?"

"What?"

"I do think he'll get better. And you know why? - Because I pray for him every night. Are you praying for your brother?"

"Honey, are we almost ready?" Dad asks Mom. "Dinner starts in fifteen."

TRANSCENDENCE - - - - Brandon aged 11 - - - - 1996

My red cummerbund rises up my waist like tides of the red sea. It practically reaches my chest. I don't know how 007 keeps his shirt so smooth. Dad's shirt is smooth too. Maybe if I sit up straight.

Man, I can't wait for the next coarse. Linguini. Oh here, yep here's the waiter. I can't wait. That looks delicious.

"Mom, would you please pass the pepper?"

I scoop my fork through lightly peppered spaghetti strands, stab a piece of boneless chicken and roll it around until I eye a full bite. Open. Chew. But after the first chew, the spicy pepper makes me cough. I cough again. *Oh no, it's not just a cough.* My oxygen erratically switches from easy rhythmic flow to jarring gasps. Losing control over my body, I slip from the dining room seat to the carpet, slicker than a waterslide.

Lying there, back on the floor, experiencing another seizure, I struggle to breathe. I close my eyes hoping to end the moment, but I notice other things, like the ship. The motion of the ship. Heavy sways.

I feel a numbing pain in my stomach. I look down to see. A glossy, black body and six straw-like legs is what I see. I'm not on the cruise ship. And I'm an ant.

"Oh my queen!" I shout out, instinctively. I shut my eyes. *What's happened here?*

The scorpion's stinger sticks straight through my abdomen.

Where was the scorpion? I didn't see it coming; but it had surely speared me like a barbequed shish kabob. Shock. Oh if it weren't for this nuisance in my stomach! Oh why? My ant body gyrates uncontrollably by motion from the scorpion's tail, but I personally can't move. I feel my body pulsate as my legs start to sprawl outward, my lower legs, my middle legs, my upper legs. I feel stiff. I can't bear to move. My antennas don't even move. *Am I dying?* "Oh Queen," I gasp.

I force my eyes open wide to witness the reality of the situation. The tip of the stinger gurgles, ready to drip a drop of venom. The drop looks bigger than my head. I wish I could pinch off the stinger and free myself. I want to live. I know it's a struggle collecting food and leaves, but it's worth it. I have things I want to do. And I need to be with Molly. The siblings said I would go first. They never thought I was a good navigator.

The tip of the stinger drips and the venom drop drips toward me, almost in slow motion, and eventually splashes my face. It's acidic. I feel the burn. My mouth opens slightly as I squirm. I tilt my head to the side and my eyes start to shut, fading.

*

"Tiempo siesta, mi amor." – The soothing voice so cozy.

*

Years of Madre's soothing voice has filled my head with life and wisdom, making me the confident Mayan man I am today. That was her intent when she named me Kul after our flying god, Kukulcan. That was her intent when she pointed out my strengths, that I can always see the big picture, keeping destiny in mind. Most people don't know their place in the world. That's what Madre says. Just look at the Aztecas. Building temples dedicated to the sun. What ignorant peons. They have no idea.

Madre says I'm destined to be among the gods, flying through the cosmos. She's always known that, and confidently. She said she had a dream as a young girl, about me, her future son. And now is the time. Right here, on this field. This ball under my foot represents the sun. Am I going to make my mark in the cosmos or not? Or like the slaved Aztecas, am I going to repeat life on earth? I know I'm ready to compete for the gods. I'm ready to compete against the gods. I'm going for it – the upper echelon.

A defender comes at me, but I shuffle my feet and spin around him like an agile jaguar. I maintain possession of the ball. I hear the fans shouting. They know I'm on my way. Two more defenders start at me. They don't realize how unthreatening they are. As they get closer, I fake like I'm going at one of them, then I flinch at the other, then I dodge between them. I maintain possession of the ball, the sun. I must protect it. The fans cheer on.

Stick to the game plan. I just need to surpass the earth level. Then I can die with satisfaction. Otherwise, after the sacrifice, I will be created here again. I dribble on and almost lose my footing in a dip in the ground. Come on, see. I'm near the center of the field and the goal is clearly in range. *Wait. Should I go for a win or should I go for the fifth level? Why am I hesitating? When King chops my head off, decapitating my earthly body, which will give me happiness? I'm not scared to die, I don't think.* I think I'm ready and the fans see that. They are up on their feet in anticipation. They cheer, "Kul, Kul!"

"Brandon!" "Brandon!" "Wake up!" "Brandon!"

I hear mom's voice. Mom, Dad and Chelsea are up out of their chairs to see to me. I feel their love. The captain and some of his crew are out of their chairs as well. "Sweetie, you had us so worried," mom says.

My palms are sweaty. Did I pass out? The dining room seems brighter. The chandeliers haven't changed. I guess the lighting is the same. Things don't feel as elegant as before. Everyone is interested. Even people at other tables look over here. The waiter is back, holding a pitcher of water.

"You had another seizure, Brandon," Mom says.

"I did, just now?" I ask in a haze.

"Oh, sweetie," Mom says again.

"Don't do that anymore," Dad jokes, but doesn't hide his worry.

"Do you know you were talking," Chelsea chimes in. "Who were you talking to?"

"I don't… It was a dream… I can't remember…"

~ ~ ~

CHAPTER 5IVE

When it happened, when insignificant dust particles extracted from microscopic cells, and also from separate bits of oxygen, and also from the rest of the atmosphere, was when I realized the material world dissolved yet again. It was a graceful waking.

It's also when I arrived at the sentiment of "alas!" and not just because I'd come to a place where the concept of eternity fits the big picture, and the small picture; and not just because of the relieving, repeating, happy epiphany sensation; but because my previous life as Chelsea finally felt dignified.

Greeted with the afterlife again, never before have I felt so dignified in my lifelong pursuits as Chelsea. Brandon's thoughts finally revealed, I was granted empathy towards him. I decided he too had transcended, and apparently into ants as well as people.

Among the afterlife, I was in a good place, where I concerned myself with eternal harmony. At the same time, I knew Chelsea's thoughts as if they used to be my own. So whatever my new purpose was meant to be, for the moment, I knew I was allowed to blissfully ponder.

An electric charge inside Brandon's brain surely triggered his transcendence. I recalled that seizure during the Panama cruise being his last. I also remembered that afterwards, doctors determined he was free from his childhood epilepsy, yet from that point on, he was 'distracted' ninety percent of the time, for the rest of his life. That's when we lost him.

After a lifetime of unyielding curiosity, and finally getting a glimpse of Brandon's perspective, the only question was: *Why*? Why was it that as this aura, and Brandon as a boy, we were traveling "transcenders?"

Given a new, unconcealed opportunity, I transcended into Brandon as a boy again. The orbiting pull lightened. I connected with his aura…And, into his body…

TRANSCENDENCE - - - - - Brandon aged 12 - - - - 1997

Portland rain, Portland rain won't wash away my stains, no not my stains.
I could have the rap game as easy as I have this ball game.
Call me Busta Bucket. And right now, this driveway is my stage.
No problem for a cross over. No problem for a fade-away.
Easy as a green light. Easy as an open mic. Yeah, I'm that tight.

All of the sneaker foot-prints prove it. So do these scattered bounce marks.

After throwing up the ball again, it's an ugly bank off the fiberglass, but it goes in. It's cool. I'll take it. I rebound the ball, pull up and fire again. After it bricks off the rim, I make another hasty recovery, a Charles Barkley worthy rebound, muscling away from imaginary defense. A thought about Barkley flashes across my mind as I retreat to the top of the key. The thought that Barkley has said he hated to practice when he was my age, but that it was worth it, to sacrifice a couple of hard years in order to be a pro.

I'll put in the work. They all did. MJ practiced in his driveway every night, like me. But for me, I'm going to be more like Bo Jackson, a two sport man. Yeah, I'm that good.

"Hey Brando," I hear Dad say as he walks down the porch. I snatch up the ball, shoot again and miss.

"What up Dad?"

"It's time for tennis."

"Finally!"

"I blame your mother."

If only it was time for tennis. If only I could stop these daydreams. I won't get to play. I won't be able to. I'll try, but then I'll zone out. Just before I do, Mom and Dad will show me looks of disappointment.

Then they'll scoot me off to the side and let me do my thing. They'll help me dribble the ball for a little while, before they go hit. Then somehow, we'll wind up back here, and I might as well not even go.

We never talk about it because everyone's already trying to fix me.

It's not fair. It's not…

It's alright. Stay positive. You can cure yourself, Brando. You can already stay in the moment sometimes. Dribbling helps. Maybe start out with the dribbling today.

TRANSCENDENCE - - - - Dan aged 51 - - - - 1997

"What's on your mind Brando," I ask glancing at him in the rear view mirror. He's checking out the rackets next to him. There's a long pause before he answers.

Brandon mumbles a question about role models. *What did he say?*

"Sure role models are good," I guess at an answer. "I've told you before that Walter Cronkite was my role model. He had integrity, stability and objectivity." *Good, Dan, keep things intellectual. It will help.*

Does Brandon have role models? Does he grasp the concept? He must. That's good too.

Suddenly jarred away from my wandering thoughts, there's a speed trap ahead.

"Radar," Brandon says, spotting the squad car which hides behind the bushes. *I just don't get his levels of awareness.*

"Those pesky police are trying to inhibit our tennis," Laurie jokes.

"Hey Brando."

No answer.

"Brandon?"

Again, nothing.

I look in the rear view mirror and see Brandon stare out the window at the intersection as we turn left. He seems gone again, his focus miles away. *The hell can we do?*

Again I call out, "Brandon?"

Silence.

"So honey, I had a great shoot today," I tell Laurie, diverting from personal despair.

"Nice dear," she says, always encouraging when I get involved in photography.

"Yeah, nice Dad," Brandon says from the back.

My ears perk and my eyes glance in the mirror again.

"Thanks Brando."

No reply.

Well it's something. We'll just keep finding things that help. If he's around more people...Yes, we'll keep traveling.

"So guys, I was thinking about another trip, another cruise. This one takes three and a half weeks through the Mediterranean."

TRANSCENDENCE - - - - Brandon aged 13 - - - - 1998

Stepping out onto the roof, the evening air is balmy. It tranquilizes my agitations. I take one shoe off and place it in the edge of the doorway to prevent the heavy door from closing. It may lock if I let it shut. There's a small red sign on it that states it's against hotel policy to be up here, but I need some alone time and our driveway is on the other side of the world.

Wearing only one shoe, I do a lopsided walk toward the edge of the building, the city view subject to my inspection, Athens.

My fretting fades a little more as I catch sight of the scene. From one of the tallest skyscraper hotels, it's as if I'm perched in the middle of creation, white-washed architecture below; I can almost sense the heavens. From here they seem reachable. It's humbling.

Who knows, maybe my quandary will be answered by a holy sign.

Although, how could my life have any purpose? My focus just gets worse. And even if I could focus, I can't focus on my sports because we travel so much. At this rate, I'm going to be an explorer instead of an athlete. But why…Why all the daydreams of athletes?

"Don't worry," I tell myself, looking across the sprawling metropolis of Athens

Looking about the city, I see it all, gas stations, pawn shops, apartment buildings, offices, other fancy hotels, homes in the hillsides, and temples dedicated to the old Grecian gods, mostly all of it white-washed.

There's little if any wasted space. Pools occupy rooftops of other hotels, and billboards stand upon some of the smaller buildings. One billboard in particular, just across the street on top of a glass blowing factory, catches my eye because it's unique, and it moves. It's made up of rotating, triangular pillars, sporting a different advertisement every thirty seconds.

First an image of the new Nokia cell phones covers the rotating triangles. *I love playing that game, Snake, on those phones –When I can focus that is.*

An ad for gas appears across the billboard next. The text is written in Greek block lettering, but the picture of a woman filling up her car makes the message clear. I wait until the billboard's triangles rotate again and the third ad sends chills down my spine.

It locks me in a trance. The third ad is for a Nike soccer campaign, a player kicking a ball into the goal. The plain white swoosh in the bottom corner, which is stretched across the last two rotating triangles, flashes at me. I know it, just as I know it's not meant to flash. It's just regular billboard poster with no lights and no glitter, but it's definitely flashing. It's baiting me. Something about it is so enchanting. It's ghostly, maybe godly.

Am I zoning out again? Am I delusional now too? Who knows? It's the Nike goddess for all I know. My shivers deepen as I once again remind myself of my athletic aspirations. I feel this buzz inside. My heart hears, "come-hither". *Really, is this a sign? Nike?*

As a native of Portland, Oregon, headquarters to Nike Inc., I grew up with the Nike story. Sometimes I like to pretend it's true, that the legend which started when the Nike goddess gave wings to the feet of a messenger, helping him finish a marathon run back to Greece to pronounce "victory" with a dying breath, lives on through the Bill Bowerman, Phil Knight, Steve Prefontaine driven clothing company. The Swoosh, Nike's logo and symbol to the wings of victory, can help any athlete fly.

REEEMMMIIITTTTTTTTTTTTTTTTTT

What? What was that?

My mental crusade is interrupted when the billboard rotates to the Nokia phones again. My heart is still feeling dazzled, but my head is grateful for the break. *I need a reality check.* The billboard rotates another time to the lady filling up her car. Collecting myself, I should get back to the room, my family.

A lopsided walk back to the door.

Lasting residue of that inner buzzing has me look one last time. The Nike soccer advertisement is there again, but the Swoosh in the corner is flat.

REEEMMMIIITTTTTTTTTTTTTTTTTT…
…buzz…

~ ~ ~

CHAPTER 6IX

A bizarre, vibrating voice accompanied me as I transcended back into the place of the afterlife.

REEEMMMIIITTTTTTTTTTTTTTTTTT

It wasn't Brandon's voice.

REEEMMMIIITTTTTTTTTTTTTTTTTT

Was this guidance?

I radiated in the buzzing feeling, intrigued that I was possibly in the presence of another. I felt as though I was closer to whatever powerful source I was orbiting. The pull was stronger.

REEEMMMIIITTTTTTTTTTTTTTTTTT

UNTILLLL

YYYOU

KNOWWWW

Who it was 'puppeteering' these spoken tremors I still didn't know, but I loosely understood the commandment. That Nike Swoosh. That was me. I wasn't sure how I did that, but that was almost beside the point. While transcending into Brandon's aura, I somehow tapped into the aura of that environment too. Hence, the Nike Swoosh.

I thought maybe Brandon was looking for a sign. Somehow I reached out.

I wondered about the commandment, 'UNTIL YOU KNOW' - *until I knew what?* I didn't seem to know much.

I knew I was amazed by Brandon's ambitions. He clearly tried to understand his own visions and live out a regular existence. I knew the feeling.

Then, before receiving any more direct answers, I transcended into mom again. In doing so, I experienced some of the answers that I seeked.

TRANSCENDENCE - - - - Laurie aged 42 - - - - 1998

As room-key cards are inserted into the cruise ship's machine, every disembarking passenger is counted as we venture off, my family included. How exciting to finally see Jerusalem and the Garden of Gethsemane. I keep holding my breath in anticipation.

Snarled in congestive city traffic, the bus we boarded at the pier can't go fast enough. I'm little Charlie, waiting to see inside of the chocolate factory.

When we finally arrive at the Garden of Gethsemane, stone walls stand tall, separating a chaotic city from preserved holy grounds. Bus loads of other tourists, engrossed in their own vacation experience, are slowly making their way inside the garden.

After exploring a cathedral within the garden, and strolling along its gorgeous paths, I find myself desperate to pause at the base of an old tree. I reach toward one of its branches, anxious to hold one of the leaves. *Could HE have touched this very branch?*

If I could see the things this tree has seen, would I be better enlightened for it? The idea has me enthralled so much that I imagine Jesus at the end of his life, and I feel deep sadness and dread.

Then, miraculously, and to my surprise, I'm lifted off the ground. A hand reaches beneath me as if from someplace high like the sky. I am lifted above the grove. It happened too fast to second-guess.

I can see the city of Jerusalem teeming with people. They look busy with their lives. They're minding their own business, but that's what's annoying. Actually it's infuriating. *Don't they know? How can they be so unaware?* I want to yell at them, at all of them. They need a preaching to. And from up here, I could easily…Mid thought, I realize it's me who I'm upset with. I haven't been living the way I ought to be.

And immediately, I am reinstated to my family and the group of tourists swarming through these holy grounds. Fear replaces the unexpected bitter-sweet setting from which I have just returned. So many people don't try, or maybe they don't know, but I can no longer brush my faith off as a nice, little Sunday-School lesson to be filed away, ready to be taken out and dusted off only on days preordained by the church calendar.

~ ~ ~

CHAPTER 7EVEN

The same harmonic voice as before:

GGGGGUUUUAAAAARRRRDDDDIIIIAAAAAN NNNSSSSSSS

I heard the response in pulsating reply to my shocked thoughts. *Guardians?*

These so-called Guardians communicated with me, Chelsea's aura, revealed some of their regular doings within the last in-body experience into Laurie.

"Helping my mom arrive to the personal affirmation of faith like that, that's what you do?" I questioned the Guardians. "Is that, like the work of angels?" It was certainly miraculous from a human point of view.

SSSSEEEEEECCCCCUUUURRRRREEEEEE

TTTTTHHHHHEEEEEE

BBBAAAAALLLLLAAANNNCCCEE

Then as if uploading new information into my conscious, I somehow knew that the Guardians interrelate with environments on earth when deemed necessary to keep balance among the universe. But I wondered, what balance? And in what circumstances do they show?

Considering the ripple effect, these interrelations could be anything.

The clairvoyant Guardians followed with:

AAAAAAAALLLLLLLLLLL

IIIIIIIISSSSSSSSSSS

CCCCCCCOOONNNNNEEEEECCCCCCTTTTT EEEEEDDDDDDD

The words hummed, already gaining a familiar palpability. To know I wasn't alone was comforting. It seemed to help me detach even more from the earthly world.

That being said, I transcended again as I steadily learned my own role in securing the balance of the universe.

TRANSCENDENCE - - - - Dan aged 52 - - - - 1998

That's enough. I have to get out of here. I turn back and frantically scurry out of the tunnel. Brandon, Chelsea and Laurie can continue inward with the rest of the group, but I just can't take it. Brandon probably doesn't know where he is, so I'm sure he'll be fine. There's the entrance where we came from, fresh air. And, I'm out. Oxygen, OK!

Two unoccupied camels are tied up near the Sphinx. More tour guides lead other tour groups around other pyramids. Depressingly, the warm desert air, open skies and bright sunshine don't come as a relief. I'm disappointed really. Travel all the way to the Sahara, but I'm not ready to stick myself in a coffin. Nope, I'll have to leave it for King Tut and the rest of the tourists.

TRANSCENDENCE - - - - Chelsea aged 11
- - - - 1998

As if in sort of a walking train, the four of us line up in single file along with our luggage and attempt to walk on planks temporarily suspended over the flooded courtyard of St. Mark's square. Elegant buildings and a cathedral encircles the courtyard like pristine walls around the world's dining room. Thousands of pigeons hop like frogs around water's edge, restaurant entrances and rooftops. Venice is our last playground before we head home. That's what

Dad says. And the almanac said Venice is a city of love, but I only feel sad. I don't want to leave Europe. I want to name it as my favorite place ever.

"Mom, can we stay here?"

"We are staying here," she answers.

"No, I mean, let's live here," I say hoping to postpone our life back home.

I can definitely picture myself living here. I mean, the streets are canals, which is so cool. I'm sure Dad would love to commute to his station by boat. I would surely find a nice Italian boy to take me for gondola rides.

"Wouldn't that be nice," she says without even a head turn, whimsically dismissing my idea. *Fine. Be like that. What do I know? I'm just a child.*

Like fairytales, no one in the family wants the vacation to end. In all the fun, and new people, and new ways of living, our vacations make Brandon's condition not matter. And Mom and Dad act like that's true too. But for some reason we always have to go back home.

Of course, we don't always know what he sees, but at least we are all together.

Back home, there are always appointments and homecare. His sleep patterns must be charted. Things he says have to be recorded.

I keep records too. I had a secret diary, but when I accidently told mom, she said I shouldn't worry. But I told her that I'm going to help. And to be guessed what, I got a digital tape recorder for my birthday.

Brandon spends most of his time in the driveway bouncing either a tennis ball or a basketball. I follow him around anyway. I think he likes it.

Then the canals, the buildings, the sky, the people, and Chelsea all start to soften like watercolors evaporating.
Buzzzzzzzzzzzzzzzzzzzzzzzzzzzzzzzzzzzzzzzzzzzzz z….

~ ~ ~

CHAPTER 8IGHT

Color! Colors in the physical universe illuminated, but here in the afterlife, colors livened. If every bit of buzz was a different speck, each was a different pigment. Beautifully diverse, each was different from the next. Dazzling! One speck blushed of deep purple and then brightened to bright pink, framed by a glowing golden corona. Another spec buzzed from turquoise to sky blue, again framed by a glowing golden corona. The glittery specs sparkled individually like trillions of fireflies, and all together, floated like silk in the wind as the buzz prevailed. This was the source, the strengthening passion that drew in my aura. This was iridescence.

What I heard was a soothing ambiance of sounds linked with innocent memories: the breath of fresh, mountain air whooshing along the powdery ski slopes, a humming sound the piano key made just after I tried playing it as a child, the free flowing tremble of ukulele strings during my first ever strums, and the whistle of a bamboo flute playing background music in those experimental yoga classes. I caught the beauty in being able to try something for the first time, as a human, and here.

How grateful I was for being graced with this enlightenment, being able to absorb the buzzing with increased awareness. I sensed with increased senses. I buzzed on all ends of the spectrum, with warmth, with dedication, with eagerness, with wrath, and everything in-between.

My existence was becoming one and the same with this rich source of life. There was so much more LIFE than I had known earlier. For this reason alone, I was less and less attached to my worldly burdens. Not only that, but there's a hovering intelligence.

As if each colorful speck was optional brain power, the source was accessible creativity. Even one percent optimization meant the capability to achieve anything. Overall, it meant that through this buzzing energy, everything was indeed connected.

On elemental levels of understanding, I grasped the concept of the physical universe, and that my life as Chelsea was a journey of desired empathy. In my case, transcending out of body was my trek back home. I didn't want to let go, but truly experiencing the perspectives of others as I transcended into various in-body experiences was the reach and the grasp of empathy. Meeting with the guardians and hearing their comforting voice was the best way for the source to be revealed to me. Transcending further, I knew that before fully joining the source, one essential thing remained.

I had transcended from Chelsea to Chelsea's aura to the joining of a being of collective consciousness. Every word spoken from here showed up in the world, somewhere, in places, or people, or actions.

Any miracle on earth started here, from hands coming out of the sky lifting Laurie up over the city of Jerusalem to the hands of a doctor lifting up a newborn.

The collective consciousness is the aura to all.

Then, as energy from the collective consciousness, and with specific intentions, another transcending experience into Brandon happened. It was another visit to his side of creation.

TRANSCENDENCE - - - - Brandon aged 14 - - - - 1999

The locker room feels deathly cold after cuts are posted.

I thought I was more than just a one sport man, but my Bo Jackson-like future, flying from a master's tennis tournament off to my Blazer games, seems like a childhood dream.

Bo stood out among his peers like an artist before his time. I can't even stand out at tryouts. I don't even try well. "Is this really…"

"…Na, ya know what Brando - aint there yet. Jordan dealt with cuts. Who's better at their sport than Jordan? Adversity is all part of it. I got this. I'll be back next year."

TRANSCENDENCE - - - - Brandon aged 15 - - - - 2000

What a practical name, - suicides; no time to think, - non-stop sprinting. I feel like I'm back in my epilepsy days. I'm running out of oxygen, killing myself here just trying to be faster than these other chumps. I either burn rubber or my spot on the team vanishes like last year. My heart pounds like a drum. Come on stay with it. Faster! OK. Just as I think I'm gaining position, I get light-headed and in the midst of sprinting all out down the waxy gym floor, my vision goes black.

*

The pack moves sleeker now - faster and quieter. The pups look like they're ready to start panting any moment. The temperature in the mountain air has dropped so our coats have puffed out like chinchillas.

Recalling father's technique to prevent the snow from sticking, I move with as much grace as possible. We weave in and out of birch trees as we run.

Though the pups are getting tired, the more we run, the more alive I feel. The balmy winter air refreshingly fans my coat as I move. Each stride is like gliding, a full stretch as I barely put a paw down on firm ground. As soon as I do, all of my muscles flex as I spring off the ground and then stretch again, momentum propels me further. I run in the same tracks that father makes, but I notice the pups in front of me miss steps. "Woof." (I'll pass you if you don't keep up) I know they heard me, but they ignore me and race on. At least they try. They still make too many tracks.

Brother steps on a branch which broadcasts a loud crack echoing through the woods. Upset, I leap over the blunderer, and land right beside him. But instead of teaching him a lesson in discipline, I slightly lose my balance, walloping my right side against a tree trunk. I brush past, but I feel bits of bark clinging to my hind leg. "Keep up," I bark at brother. I can't believe father didn't turn around. Maybe he keeps going because we need this hunt.

I feel like giving the pups more incentive, "I'm eating everyone smaller than me if we don't get this Bison." I love Bison. Right then I feel a harsh bug bite. I stop and turn, revealing fangs to chew at the patch of skin newly roughed up by bark. There must be a bug. I'll get it, a snack before we gorge on Bison. Bark bits fall off into the snow as I gnaw more. That hurt. I find the bite mark and rub my nose against it. It's already bloated into a hefty bump. I think a spider got me, but I can't find him; lucky little foe. I better catch the up with the pack.

I swing my head forward ready to sprint up to the pack, but my head feels light and my eyes feel heavy. My vision is woozy. Go. Go. I can't pick up any momentum. My progress seems to be more sideways than forward. "Keep marching at least." Snow and trees and nightfall start meshing together. "Oh no! Venom must be flowing through my veins."

The blurred pack furthers on. Do they know I stopped? I'm struggling here. I'm missing more steps than the pups. I can't keep going. Pant. Pant. Now who's panting? Don't tease yourself, come on. I'm going to be left behind. If the pack keeps on, I'll be lost forever - this isn't our terrain. My brothers and sisters always teased me that I would be first to get lost. They accused me of being cursed. "Lone wolf," they say. It's because I'm the oldest and... I feel so alone. Drop. Collapse in the bitter cold.

Squeak! I'm back at tryouts. I'm still running suicides alongside my fellow basketballers, rubber soles pound against gymnasium wood. I'm actually in remarkable position, leading everyone else. I'm fast! However, as I acknowledge their presence, they start to catch me. Now passing. "Come on Christopher, move," a coach yells from the sidelines. *Let's go BC, push yourself. Keep going. Stay Awake!*

We cross the half court line several more times, but I'm not fast enough. I'm too stressed over this stupid condition. We go over dozens of fundamental drills, but my game isn't clean enough. My head isn't clear enough. We do several shooting exercises, but I don't make enough shots. High school tryouts are the extent of my basketball career. Cuts are the finale.

I remember relating to Bo Jackson last year. I'm not sure why. The dude is, over six feet tall, 220 pounds of iron. He's probably the strongest, fastest, and most athletic player of his era, in both of his sports. Even if my head was screwed on straight, I'm 5'3, weighing a buck thirty. Technically I'm three inches taller than I was last year; but still, the shortest guy on the team doesn't play, not to mention the craziest.

I'll understand the coach's decision. But obviously I've had more than just a deep seeded feeling that I'm supposed to be an athlete. If only I could just freaking focus.

Well thanks anyway, Bo. Maybe it's tennis.

"Dinner," Mom calls from the kitchen window.

I take one last shot. The ball banks off the backboard and rolls down the driveway into the lawn. *I'll get it later.*

Wait, wait.

Did I just dream all that? I'm in the driveway?

Oh I can't be that crazy!

~ ~ ~

CHAPTER 9INE

Buzzzzzzzzzzz…

TRANSCENDENCE - - - - Laurie AGED 46 - - - - 2002

Oh well. We all have the tendency to wander when we're in new places. I guess the Tretyakov Gallery is no different. I'll find them later. I hope one of them is watching after Brando. This painting captivates me.

This is the way it is you know. This is what happened. The artist didn't think. He had the oils, the brushes and the canvas, but those were just his tools. The real genius was in his head. He took his hand armed with a brush, reached back into his head, and brought it out. He delivered his energy straight to us on canvas.

He took the bit of reality around him - the mongrels beneath the table fighting each other for the drumstick that had accidentally fallen, the miserable wenches too poor to fix their torn blouses serving them tankards of ale, the obese lord wiping his greasy mouth with the back of his hand for lack of a napkin - and he made all that bleak reality into beauty. He didn't think; he just became one with his brush.

I wonder if that's a part of God's plan - the oneness.

~ ~ ~

CHAPTER 10EN

TTTTTTTHHHHHHEEEEEEEEE

OOOOONNNNNNNNNNNEEEEEEENNNNNEEEESSSSSSSSSSS

It whirred in our senses of the collective consciousness before it had surfaced as Laurie's recent thoughts.

Next, our collective consciousness played out through Brandon.

TRANSCENDENCE - - - - Brandon AGED 16 - - - - 2002

I wish the whole tournament could be erased from my memory - from the beginning until my loss - From the moment 64 ego-boosted junior players showed up and signed in, strapped with Prince or Wilson or Babolat backpack racket bags the size of body bags filled with several rackets, water bottles, energy bars, towels, extra shirts, strategy books and any other tool that might help earn an honest win, to the moment that half of the tournament field is disenchanted and eliminated after the first round.

No matter what equipment I pack, I can't seem to bring my wits. I'm off in 'storyland' for most of a matches.

Tennis is all I have at this point, and failing at it is failing at all I have. Fuming with frustration, I could just explode.

Racket in hand, twisting at the core, I swing my right arm down and back behind me, up, and then heave it forward onto the parking lot concrete. The frame snaps at the top of the racket and the strings lose tension.

I lift and smash the racket on the ground again. I lift it up and smash it again. I do it again and again and again.

Smash.

Smash.

Smash.

It feels good to get out the rage.

I let the racket dangle, like the pom-pom of the losing team's cheerleader.

OK. Compose yourself. I straighten my posture and inhale a deep, stress relieving breath.

I know better than destroying my equipment. It's not proper etiquette nor respectful. But all of this pressure is starting to boil. I feel like I've been cooking with a recipe that calls for bubbling desires and extra disappointments. Breaking a racket is the most appropriate side dish. It just is. It goes better than therapy. I can dismiss a racket like leftovers. I'll throw it away in a forlorn garbage can on the walk home. I think there's one behind that restaurant.

I've got enough rackets to spare one for an occasional stress reliever, if that's what it takes.

Or what if I quit?

I could.

Statistically it's supposed to take 10,000 hours of practice to get good enough anyway. I'm already behind, and with my mind, who knows if I'll ever catch up? I probably won't.

But then again, it's the only thing that keeps me somewhat sane.

I'm getting better.

I don't know what it is, but if I keep dribbling, it helps.

… "Brando, Big Man, your' mom is too good. Let's head home, eh?" Dad scoops up the rackets and water bottles. "Good game, honey."

"Anytime you want a rematch," Mom stirs.

TRANSCENDENCE - - - - Brandon AGED 18 - - - - 2003

I'm stressed, running a little late. I zoom, dodging traffic. I pretend red lights are yellow lights, ignoring rules of the road.

Come on, get there.

Thinking about: The college coaches who scout players from this tournament; The last match, and how well I played; The confidence that helped me; The confidence boosters.

After putting my own butt to the grindstone on the practice court, and honestly after all of the helpful dribbling, mom and dad gave me an awesome gift for Spring Break - a week's training at the Nick Bollettieri Tennis Academy in Bradenton, Florida. I already read brochures about the academy - a tennis school where legendary pros like Andre Agassi, Jim Courier, Tommy Hass, and Xavier Malisse earned their stripes. Those players attended the academy as full timers for years at a time. Even though I only had a week, I took advantage.

It wasn't really a spring vacation. It was more like a highly intensified version of the work I had already been doing, but for me, it was like heaven. Opportunity. Tennis filled the air thicker than Florida's humidity. The academy consisted of fifty plus courts of multiple surfaces, a state-of-the-art gym, a video analysis center, a nutrition center, and on and on. Pros and soon to be pros walked to and from courts like weekend warriors walked around my tennis club at home. I learned from world renowned coaches and sparred against their protégé players who were on their way to the top of the game.

The greatest bit of information that I took away from my experience at the Bollettieri academy, what got me to a collegiate level, is that a dominant player must have a dominant weapon. It can be intelligent shot making, speed, a fast serve, or maybe a big forehand. Whatever it is though, the weapon is a crucial aspect in consistently winning - if nothing else, it at least ensures winning more points in a game and more games in a match.

I always knew speed could be my weapon, but hopefully I can avoid getting caught for it here in traffic, and still get there on time.

C'mon, focus!

Zoom.

Then electrons and energy…

~ ~ ~

CHAPTER 11LEVEN

TRANSCENDENCE - - - - Chelsea AGED 17 - - - - 2004

Before I could get ready to leave for the pool, the captain gurgles a message over the intercom that whale pods are just meters from the starboard side. He says the whales are easily visible from the ship's spacious promenade level. "Spacious promenade level," I mockingly repeat. *What are we on the Price is Right? It sounds like the captain has been spending*

too much time with the effervescent cruise director. You don't have to sell the whales, buddy.

Despite the TV-commercial tone of his announcement, it works like a piper's call. The majority of the passengers on board are already in the ship's furnished halls, in the elevators and in the stairwells rushing past each other like they are doing the bathroom hustle; quickly, but not too quickly because after all, we are still on a cruise. Excitement is in the air. It's a wonder the ship doesn't tip over on its side. Maybe the captain should have told the even numbered cabins to go starboard and the odd numbered ones to go portside. Heh, heh, heh.

We too head for the whales. It's not every day that one gets to see Earth's largest mammals. *They may even be larger than those fancy umbrella drinks on the Lido Deck.*

Lucky for Dad, he already has his camera in hand because he just finished taking one of the cruise's digital photo classes.

"I figure it best to get to a lower level," Dad says. "We'll be closer to the water and we can ditch most of the crowds." We head to the fourth level. It's normally dedicated to the eighty-two-year-olds in Velcro strapped shoes pumping it out on the outdoor track that spans around the ship, but right now it's about to be our prime viewing area. *I wonder how many passengers neglect our theory by following the captain's suggestion. I wonder how many decided to stay in their cozy rooms, watching the whales from their windows or balconies.*

A draft flows through the lobby because several other passengers must have indeed shared in our logic and have beaten us here. We find about fifty passengers outside already greeting the whales as Brandon holds the door for Mom, Dad, and me. "Orca" is the word of the moment. It's just as common as the visible foggy breath lifting above those chatting about the orcas. Brrrr, it's cold out here. *Glad I brought a blanket.*

Fifteen or twenty orcas swim, and splash, and blow mist into the air, in the glacier's bay. Snow capped icebergs line the edges of clean Alaskan water.

"They're so big," Mom says as we head to the railing for a front row lean. They sure are big, but I think they seem small compared to the ship.

Dad looks through his camera lens while the whales play. I hear the doors behind us as a few more passengers trickle out.

"Look, Honey, Orcas." Most passengers use their indoor voices because the moment feels special.

"Wow! Orcas!" Some are too excited to be quiet.

"Like Keiko," Brandon says.

"Yes, there are a bunch of Free Willies out there," I say. *Brando you seem good.*

"Look at that one breaching," Mom says as one whale repeatedly shoots out of the water to slap his back against the water's surface the way a grizzly bear might scratch his back against a tree.

To me, of the black and white pod, the whale most noticeable is one barely nosing above the water's surface, as if she's curious. I understand this notion. I can just imagine this whale's world – a place where sunbeams delve into the water and dance with fluidity all the way until depths are dark. To the whale, the depths are the beginning. The illuminating beams are from the air world.

From my perspective whale silhouettes move under the water in big, graceful loops. The submerged whales seem to relish the space. They swim back twists, slicing through the cold blue with stretched fins. They move at the perfect pace, as if the water is there to support these heavy creatures, to slow them, but not get in their way of enjoying a swim. When they aren't feeding, migrating, or mating, this exercise is probably their favorite thing to do.

So to be born into this swimmable environment, and then rise to the top of the water, and then just barely nose above, just to see, is curiosity. *There is another creation up here, where the air is cool, and dry, and feeds my lungs. Look at all of these things: Sky; Birds; Sun; Massive floating vessel that makes funny sounds.*

"Brando, look at that one," I say, hoping to share with him.

No answer. He's gone! *Where is he?*

All three of us turn to find Brandon sitting against the ship's outer wall with his eyes closed.

"Brando."

"Brando."

That's too bad. I mean, whales aren't an everyday thing. I go to him, crouch beside him.

"Are you there, Brando?"

"Oh Chels," mom exclaims.

It seems like he's about to come to. I lean in close. *Come back*, I pray.

He slightly rolls his head. His lips form silent figures as if he's trying to whisper. *Brandon?*

I lean in a little closer. *Brandon?* All of a sudden my eardrums are pierced as Brandon's eyes pop open and he sits upright and belts out a whale call that reaches the other passengers on deck just as fast as is it does the glaciers. *Owe!!* I fall back.

"Oh no," mom says.

I look to see all of the other passengers on this level staring at us instead of the whales. In our circumstances it's never good if we're getting attention over whales.

Mom and dad come over. A few of the other passengers step closer to us, completely uncertain. Then someone hollers, "Look!"

We all look, everyone except for Brando. The passenger points at the whales. They form a single file line and approach the ship. *What?* The first whale swims to the part of the ship closest to Brandon. The whale nudges its nose against the painted steel, and then blows mist out of its spout and then swims back to the open space to play again. The next whale in line does the exact same thing. So does the third, and the fourth. They each take their turn to give a quick pound to that spot on the ship.

Brandon hasn't moved. He isn't even visible from the water. He's still not with us consciously.

TRANSCENDENCE - - - - Dan AGED 59 - - - - 2004

I never chased the NY network dream.

Maybe I could say American Dream. I got the house and the family with 2.5 kids. Compared to the people in the third world countries we've visited, I'll be retiring like a billionaire. C'mon Dan. Is this really the time? The bills won't stop. With Brando's incident yesterday, his costs certainly aren't going anywhere. Property taxes too. Traveling. Traveling is our saving grace. We need to travel.

A full day at sea doesn't wash away the worries of the world, but the gentle rocking of the ship made for an appreciated cabin nap. *It's too bad this is our only full day at sea.*

As the cabin door swings open, Laurie appears, dressed in a sporty Puma outfit. She sits down beside the bed to unlace her shoes.

"Honey, can we leave early for the massage?" I ask. "There is something I would like to discuss with you."

She notices that I just woke up from a coma-like nap and toys with me. "Sure honey, I'm ready right now. Let's go," she says, reaching for her bathrobe. *That is the fastest she's ever been ready.*

"Very funny," I tell her in my stupor, scrambling to get myself ready. I spot the same grey sweater that I had abandoned on the edge of the chair. One sleeve droops to the floor.

I pull on the sweater, snatch my watch and room key from the dresser and slide into my loafers. Lifting my bathrobe from the hook on the closet door, I stuff it under my arm and head out. OK gym rat, let's do it."

"Where are the kids?" I ask as Laurie leads us to the spa. *I'm pretty sure it's near the fitness center. I don't know. I understand the layout of these ships with perfect timing - about the same time our vacation is over.*

"I think Chelsea met some of the performers and asked Brandon to join them," she says. "It'll be alright. Chelsea's got him." As I shake away my grogginess, I try to recall which performers, hoping Brandon will manage.

"Oh do you mean the Broadway performers from the dinner show?"

"Yeah, I think Chelsea met them at the pool," she says as she hits the elevator button. "She's so good at making friends. Hey let's take the stairs instead?" She enthusiastically says as if it's some brilliant idea.

"Oh sure, make this old man walk extra why don't you," I pretend grimace as we begin our assent up six flights of carpeted stairs.

We pass a younger couple on the first flight of the steps. "Those are the parents of the boy," I hear whispered.

Getting a bit serious I say, "Honey, what I want to talk about is my career."

I glance ahead and see the framed 40 x 60 painting that hangs on the landing against a polished mahogany wall on the first landing. It reminds me how much more I enjoy larger-sized pieces.

We wind our way higher.

"What about your career?" she asks.

"Well television news just isn't the same as it once was. It's no longer about quality. It's now all about glib teases and coaxing people to watch, even though we don't offer much worth watching. I got into this business so I could share information. And you know I can't stand our editor."

She slows a little bit and says, "Well, isn't that something you always say?"

"Well honey, even though you stay as young as when I first met you, I happen to be aging." She bounds up the next few steps, proving her superhuman youth.

"I have a decade on you, young lady," I jokingly shout. "I think I'm going to retire from broadcasting. I've been in the news business almost forty years now. The kids are growing up."

A small crowd of people pass through the lobby just above the third flight of stairs. Most of them give us looks of recognition.

Laurie waits for me and quietly asks, "What will you do?" We both try our best to ignore the spectators.

"I'm thinking photography, full time. It's a risk to jump careers, and who knows what's going to happen with Brando, but business has always been there."

"I'll support you, dear."

Just as long as I can support us too.

TRANSCENDENCE - - - - Brandon AGED 19 - - - - 2004

"I like the tennis players." Even her laugh has a Belarusian accent. "So how old are you?"

"I'm nineteen. Why, Yvonne? How old are you?"

"It is none of your business," she smirks. "I'm twenty two."

We smile at each other for a few seconds. She's got something on her mind. "So you talk with the whales, yeah?" she asks.

"No, I'm not sure."

"What do you mean you're not sure? You –"

"I know what I did. Well…I know what I did because everyone told me what I did. Sometimes I'm not always present."

"What do you mean, you are like crazy person?"

"That's the easiest way to put it. I don't know. I don't know what happened yesterday. I wasn't myself. I wasn't a whale either. I felt like I was swimming with others –"

"Other people?"

"No…just other souls, I guess. I think I yelled because I was calling out to our creator. I don't know. It's tough to explain. Weird things happen to me all the time. I understand if you don't get it."

She looks at me as though she wonders something. *I wonder if she wonders why I'm not locked away in a cage.*

"It's OK. I like crazy. My father was crazy."

She bites her lower lip as she dips beneath the roaring Jacuzzi water all the way to her nose. She comes right back up, gently swerving her wetted shoulders to show off her bikini top. "Do you like my swimsuit? It's new."

"It's not bad," I smile, somewhat trying not to host a staring contest with her swimsuit top. "So you're from Belarus. How did you wind up in New York? How did you wind up on cruise ships?"

"When I was seventeen I was offered a job on Broadway. I took it and this was good, but then I took job with Princess Cruises. I like the variety and the travel. I get to sail many places. It's good money if you count the free room and board."

"Did they give you a nice room?"

She looks right into my eyes and blinks softly the way a butterfly flaps its wings before takeoff.

~ ~ ~

CHAPTER 12WELVE

TRANSCENDENCE - - - - Brandon AGED 21 - - - - 2006

*

Car horns honk as the squad car corkscrews to a screeching stop in the middle of the intersection.

"Hey buddy!" Officer Hernandez shouts. He rushes out of the car. "Hey!"

"Was it this…? No, no, it must have… Wait, was it that way?" Disrupting traffic, Jeremy ignores Officer Hernandez and his partner, Officer Lebrun, pacing back and forth across one corner of the intersection with a tennis racket in hand.

"Hey buddy!" Officer Hernandez shouts again, approaching.

"Steve look, he's barefoot." Officer Lebrun points out. "This pavement's got to be 95 degrees."

"What's the deal with the racket?"

"I don't know. He could be on something."

"Broadway and Campbell - we have a 507 and possible 390," Officer Hernandez reports into his radio.

"I'm sure if I go... Well, which way did I come from again?" Jeremy continues to pace as the two officers approach closer.

"Hey buddy, why are you in the street?"

Noticing the policemen, Jeremy suddenly freezes. His blonde hair and Nike tennis shirt whisk in the breeze. "What are you doing here? Leave me alone. I'm very busy." He resumes his pacing.

"We can't have you in the street like this?"

"The probability of the road following west... No, it depends upon the terrain..." Jeremy mumbles.

"Hey buddy!" The officers move in closer and Jeremy freezes once again, this time tensing.

"Stay back!" He raises his tennis racket, waving it at both of the officers like a magic wand. They both reach to the tazers on their hips, ready to draw. Another squad car pulls up and Officer Zimmerman quickly jumps out.

*

"Oh no!" I gasp. "What was that? Was that Jeremy?"

Since I decided to try to make it on the pro tour instead of going to play college ball first, it's been online classes alongside an individual tennis schedule.

I want the education, and I can manage the workload, but this economics paper is so boring, it's taming my soul; and now I know something terrible has just happened to coach Jeremy.

Ungluing myself from my desk chair, I reach my arms up, failing to stretch away encumbering stresses.

"Why do I have to put up with this bullshit?"

Guys like Nadal, and Tsonga, and Berdych steadily climb the ATP rankings, while crazy Brando here, has to check his reality, and then his homework, before he can even get to practice. Some life, Brando.

Thirsting for that competitive fix that I love, the only thing that seems to help me, I focus back on the computer, minimize Microsoft Word and click on an online chess application.

John McEnroe says tennis is chess on wheels. Both tennis and chess are strategy games, that rely on intelligent decision making, and forced errors. The first side to lose his wits usually loses the comp.

"Alright, whatcha got chump?"

I open with a traditional move - king's pawn up two spaces. My randomly matched opponent, WIZKID73, mirrors my move. I bring out a knight. WIZKID73 brings out the opposite knight. I backup my leading pawn with another pawn. He and I move at the same pace shifting our virtual pieces around creating ready opportunity to attack. After eight moves by both sides no pieces have been killed off, but a war wages.

It's like a tennis match as if we're tied at four all in the first set and neither of us have been able to break the other's serve.

Being the first to take a lead is probably what I concern myself with more than anything. It's my first priority in tennis. I want to be the first to control a point. As I make a few more moves in the chess game, I think about my tennis life for the past few years. I think about where my head has been, the progress I've made.

Coach Jeremy and I have worked together for a little while now. He was a mutual friend of one of my former coaches back in Portland. Most importantly, we relate to each other real well. He struggles with the mind too.

Eight years older than me, he's not only a role model because of the way he handles a certified bipolar condition, but he's one of the brightest minds I know. He admits he's crazy, but so do I.

His methods are a bit unorthodox, but improvements in my game are noticeable and it seems I receive acknowledgements from other coaches and players on a daily basis. He instills a certain confidence in me.

In the past few years I had upped my training. I had gone back to the Bollettieri Academy in Florida. I had gone to another academy in Texas, the John Newcombe Tennis Ranch. I spent time traveling and competing with dozens of up and coming pros. But nothing is comparable to a court session with Jeremy.

He'll drill me on one shot for four hours straight, until I have it down perfect. Then he'll have me skip rope for another half an hour while he stands by and unloads his philosophy on me. Sometimes it's just his philosophy on life, but somehow it helps my tennis.

"Tennis is not just about tennis," he'll say. "Master one art form in order to gain the keys to many."

Jeremy makes statements like this every time we work together. And after most practice sessions or matches, when we grab lunch, his helpful tidbits and interesting perspectives pour out of him. It's like sitting there with Yoda.

Often times during lunch, he pulls out a portable chess board and sets it up right on the restaurant table. Then he beats me and says, "Again."

I try again and he says, "Would you lose focus that fast on the tennis court?" or "You don't see all of the options." I'm constantly being worked on, and it makes me feel as though I'm on the right path. More than anything, he helps me to keep my focus.

The daydreams are fewer now, except of course, this last daydream specifically about Jeremy. *Can't be good.* It's all so frightening. My reality tessellates together like an MC Escher draws my life. It's not fair. I really wouldn't be able to say if I was out and about, or locked away with other loonies in the crazy bin.

Speaking of reality check, the tangent distracted me from this chess game. WIZKID73 managed to sneak his knight past my borders, forking my queen, my rook and to make matters worse, puts my king in check.

Seeing only disparity in the dilemma, I'm saved from immobility when the phone rings.

"Hello?"

"Yes, I'm looking for Brandon Christopher," a deep voice states, his tone use to validity.

"Speaking."

"I'm Officer Zimmerman from the Tucson Police Department. Do you know a Jeremy Nelson? He listed you as his only contact."

As odd as it may otherwise be, I already know what this is about.

"Yes, I do. He's my coach."

"Tennis, I presume," he says.

"Yes, he's my tennis coach."

"That makes sense. We had to arrest him for attempted assault on an officer. He tried to use a tennis racket as a weapon."

"Look, Jeremy isn't violent, not normally. He's bipolar."

Sometimes the manic lapses get the better of Jeremy. But he's still my friend. And that expression about genius bordering insanity - J could be the poster child. Sometimes, he's a regular John Nash.

We're supposed to leave for another tournament soon, and it was just yesterday that we had our last practice session. Actually, it wasn't really a practice session. I met Jeremy at the Tucson Racket Club, our current hub.

He was on court 10, waiting for me. As soon as I got there and put my bag down, he handed me two different rackets. "Here, hit with both of these."

"What, at the same time? Let's get to it, jokester."

"Just hit with these and hit with both of them," Jeremy insisted.

"What do you mean both of them?"

Then as if to demonstrate, with one racket in each hand, he swirled around his arms in windmill type motions. "If you cannot play with two rackets at the same time, then you're not ready to play."

He wasn't all there. "Fuck off, let's practice."

But he didn't move. "J, come on dude."

Only by paying attention to the expression his eyes made, could I tell that he was struggling with some force beyond his control. It took an intensity to keep his eyes from wandering. It's like he was fighting to sober himself after too much to drink. I knew he was going manic.

"Hey kid," he said, trying fight off his condition. "Listen."

Wholeheartedly being able to relate, "What is it, bro?" I asked, worried.

His facial expression, stone cold, "I've given you all I can," he said. "You must go on without me." It sounded like some cliché line out of a movie.

"No, it's OK dude. You're just being dramatic. We got this. We'll help each other."

The two rackets hanging by his sides, he shook his head. "No, you cannot listen to me anymore, or anyone else. Everyone's worldview is a box and the reality is that there is no box."

"Jeremy, bro, everything is fine. What if we get your meds?" I wish I could just pop some meds to keep an even keel, but no one knows what the hell… it's fine.

I was having a conversation with myself because J wasn't listening. He put the rackets on the ground and started untying his shoes. He mumbled something, talking to the shoes. "So many are swept along by the tides, and they never stop to evaluate."

What?

Then he stood upright and looked at me in another struggle for sobriety. "Brando, this time it's too strong. I need my freedom." He picked up a racket and ran away barefooted.

I couldn't find him anywhere. I called his girlfriend. I called mutual friends. I was getting ready to call the police and ask them to put out a search, but it takes 24 hours. Apparently, that call was coming either way. *I'm just glad he's found and alright.*

Officer Zimmerman explains the situation. "Well, I heard the call over the radio and I was in the area so I turned up to assist. I've dealt with mental cases before and when I recognized Jeremy's state of mind, I alerted the other officers. Even still, they had to tazer him and arrest him for attempted assault. He's been transferred to St. Joseph's Hospital off of Wilmot Street."

I bet you've never seen a case like me, I think, writing down St. Joseph's on a notepad.

Officer Zimmerman continues, "I personally followed up just after he arrived at the hospital. He's in pretty bad shape. The doctor there did an initial evaluation and he said it's the worst case he's ever seen. They said family and friends can visit, but it will almost certainly be a long while before he gains clarity and is released."

A moment of silence passes because I'm not sure what to say. *Damn it J, what the hell?*

"Thanks for the call, officer. I'll figure it out."

~ ~ ~

CHAPTER 13IRTEEN

TRANSCENDENCE - - - - Chelsea AGED 20 - - - - 2007

Corvallis is normally nippy. I didn't realize how hot it would be, but I broke a good sweat. OK unleash. Cadet shakes her neck and then jogs to her dog bowl. I fill a glass with cold, filtered water for myself. Right as I put the glass down by the sink, my phone sends a quick vibration to the counter top. I check and it's a text from Mom. "Feel like Skype?" Now is actually a perfect time, so I shoot a message back. "Indeed."

I let myself fall into the living room lounger so I can multitask, talk with mom and veg. Cadet jumps on the sofa and nestles into a cushion. I grab my laptop off the side table and sign into Skype.

Mom already waiting online, calls before I can do anything. Answer with video. Two video screens pop up. One screen is mom, as she looks at me, wide eyed with a grin just as wide. The second screen is smaller and off to the bottom left corner. It's her view of what she sees.

"Hi Mom, why are you in a bathrobe? Did you just get up?"

"No, it's just a little chilly this morning. Humphrey is keeping me warm though. He's resting in my lap right now."

"Oh, can I see?" She lifts him slightly in front of the monitor so I can see his fluffy face peering above the dining room table.

"He looks happy."

"Yeah, he's a happy camper, but he's getting older. If I move him too much he'll turn into a grumpy old man." We laugh together.

"Mom, why the big grin?"

"Well it's just good to talk with you, sweetie. I'm sorry we missed each other last week."

"Yeah I'm sorry too. But I'm glad I did the race. It was a nice break."

"I'm so proud of you Chelsea."

"Mom," I whine.

"Well a half marathon is incredible."

"Yeah, I'm the best," I laugh. "But Cadet gets most of the credit," I say reaching over to scratch her belly. "She's been running with me every morning before class. I think I want more though. I'm going to come up and run the Portland Marathon next year."

"Really?!" Mom says in excitement.

"Yep, I've already started training."

"Oh, I can't wait to see you! You should come up this weekend."

"I can't this weekend. I have too much going on. Plus I haven't studied for midterms yet. I'll be home the weekend after for Thanksgiving break."

"I can't wait."

"How's Dad and, Brandon?"

"They are good. Dad bought some more digital software for the studio. He's been working hard. And Brandon is good too. We've been writing together."

"You have?"

Mom diligently writes Christian devotionals for St. Matt's, *but what could Brandon possibly write?*

"Yeah, Brandon and I hunker down in the dining room and write. I got a nice journal notebook for him. He's been using it."

"Wow. What does he write? I want to read it."

"I don't know. I told him it was his private journal."

"Well I want to know. Don't you think that could help us?"

"I don't care. It's just for him," Mom says sternly.

"But Mom, it could seriously help us."

"No sweetie."

"Ugh! Well I've been researching what I can. I'm not making any leg-way. Some of the professors would like to see him. Do you think we can get him down here?"

"No, I don't think that's a good idea. I'm tired of these scientists using Brando as a guinea pig. Besides, we cart him around enough as it is, with all of the traveling."

"Mom they aren't going to use him as a guinea pig. They want to help. Why is this a common argument? It's almost like you don't want to help Brandon anymore."

"I don't think it's a good idea."

"Mom, it's the only reason I'm in school," I say, mustering all of the authority I can garner.

"Darling you need to get your degree," she says patronizing me.

"Mom please," I plea. *Does she even care anymore?*

"I don't think it's a good idea. You'll have to check with your father, but he's busy right now."

"Fine, well is Brando around? Do you think he'll Skype?"

"I'm sure he will. Cassandra is in the kitchen fixing him something to eat. Let me get them." She picks Humphrey up into her right arm and carries him off with her to the kitchen. The monitor is facing the window which leaves me with a view of outside. Foliage and small branches are being patted down by drizzling raindrops. *Each raindrop is a teardrop. I'm glad it's not that crummy here.*

As Mom returns with Brandon and Cassandra, I hear their voices before I see them. "Your sister wants to say hi," Cassandra says. She helps him take a seat and stands off to the side. Mom scoots up next to Brandon in another chair.

"Hi Brando," I say trying to read his demeanor. Straight faced, he stares past me. Thinking of something to say, I catch his black, cashmere hooded sweater. Mom always buys him new outfits. Always a fresh look. His hair is recently trimmed too. He'd be a lady killer if he could function.

"That's a nice sweater." He puts his left hand on his chest just below his right collar bone and looks down, feeling the sweater. Then he looks up and inquisitively peers at me with those blue eyes.

He looks past me again. I can barely take it.

"I have to go Mom. Bye guys. Bye Brando." I close the laptop and head to my desk to study. *I need to find the answer.*

TRANSCENDENCE - - - - Brandon AGED 22 - - - - 2007

My phone buzzes back with a text from Chels. "Indeed." As soon as her screen name lights up under my buddy list I double click it and call. Two screens pop up; one with Chelsea's flat-ironed hair and smiling face, and a smaller one off to the lower right with her view of me.

Chelsea starts. "You're draped in Vandal gear I see. You sure you don't miss touring around?"

"Na, Idaho is cool. Besides I like the guys on the team here, and we travel enough."

"Any Idaho skiing?"

"Some. Definitely wish more. But what you been up to? Congratulations on finishing the half marathon."

"Thanks. It was really fun. Yeah, nothing much, just studying. The Civil War game is coming up this weekend."

"Yeah," I say checking myself out in the smaller screen.

"Brando, you know you're on camera right?"

"What?"

"I can see that you're looking at yourself."

"What?"

"Oh, my vain brother," she giggles.

I try to hide my embarrassment by changing the subject. "How have you been doing with the guys anyways?"

"A couple dates with this guy Chris." A sudden thud interrupts her response…

All three of my roommates, Rob, Tim and Joel, barge into my room, "Oh she's hot," they snort and chuckle. "Are you Brando's sister?"

"Chelsea, this is Rob, Tim and Joel," I say introducing my tennis teammates and roommates.

"I hear accents," she says. I glare at the boys.

I speak before they can. "Rob is from England. Tim is from Australia. And Joel is a fellow American. He's one of us," I teasingly whisper.

"What are you guys doing in the States," Chelsea asks.

Tim and Rob look at each other and smile. "Tennis," they say simultaneously. "Scholarship," Rob says. "Damn foreigners," Joel jokes.

"I like accents. Exotic," Chelsea says.

"Hey," I jump in. "What about this Chris?"

"What," Chelsea playfully says.

"We like you too," Tim says.

"Ok, that's enough," I say standing up. "Ladies, out of the room," I say punching Tim in the arm and push them out.

"Oi, what'd I say?" Tim exclaims.

"No more from the aliens. Out. Chels, I gotta go," I say looking back at the laptop. "We have practice soon anyways."

"Ok, have a good day. Good luck."

"See ya over Thanksgiving."

"Hey Brandon, let's go and finish lunch," Cassandra suggests, taking me back to the kitchen.

~ ~ ~

CHAPTER 14OURTEEN

TRANSCENDENCE - - - - Laurie AGED 51 - - - - 2008

The afternoon sun highlights sandy specs across Brandon's cheeks. He's starting to grow plenty of facial hair. I wonder if he shaves on his own, or if it's Cassandra. "I'm sure he can do it."

Because we cart Brandon with us all over the world, we try to keep up his appearance. Well, I do at least. That way, from an outsider's perspective, Brandon is seen as a sharply dressed, young man. It's not to hide his disorder; it just helps keep the normalcy. We've found it also reduces questions, spoken and unspoken.

Here in Africa it doesn't matter as much.

Masai children, the local tribal children, sidle next to Brando as he leans against a tree in-between two mud huts, writing in his journal. No matter where you go in the world, kids are troubled with far less baggage than the rest of us are. These kids don't care if Brandon is clean cut. They don't care if he functions in a certain way. *Kids are simple. They relate to anyone.*

Amazingly enough, Brandon seems to give them as much attention as they give him. He lets them flip through the pages of his journal. He pulls a yellow smiley face sticker out of his pocket and sticks it on the chest of one of the smaller boys. The kid stands up. Grinning bigger than the smiley face, he puffs out his chest like he's wearing an honorable medal. The kids smile too. Hating to interrupt this interaction, I reluctantly pull Brandon away because I need to help cook dinner for the rest of the missionaries and I dare not leave him alone.

"Brando, we have to go sweetie."

"Alright mom, let's call it a day," he says sustaining his coherency. That always catches me off guard, but I do love it. I wish it would last.

He stands up and so do the Masai children. He follows me to the Land Rover and the Masai children follow behind him. Stepping into the car and leaning out of the window Brandon says "Asanti" to the children, which we've learned is Swahili for 'thank you' and he waves as we drive off. They wave back and chase the car for a couple hundred feet. We only drive along the dirt road for about a mile before we reach our lodging.

As we arrive two shirtless Masai villagers are dropping off a live lamb and soda as a gift. The local minister is inside with Dan and the rest of the missionaries who converse about past trips before dinner. Our church has been doing missions here for several years, but this is the first time for Dan, Brandon and me to join a mission. Aside from helping with the ongoing projects, Dan is filming a documentary piece, which will be used for fundraising purposes, and I'm creating a theatrical play based off of our experience to bring awareness to St. Matt's church congregation back home. Our intentions are two-pronged; a chance to see Africa, and a chance to make an impact in the lives of others.

I dash into the sleeping quarters to wash up and change. The shower is one of the aspects in the house that isn't modernized engineering. It's more like a camping shower. We leave water-filled bags to hang outside each day for the sun to heat. The showerhead spreads the water that pours out of the bag like a regular shower, but it doesn't create much pressure, making it tough to scrub off the dried paint chips on my hands and arms. Reaching for the soap reminds me of the repetitive nature of painting the school's exterior walls that we did all day today. I think again of the school kids inside. The kids were writing their homework problems out on the dirt floor with sticks made of old tree branches they found.

Entering back into the kitchen which opens around the dining area, I survey the table noting what else needs to be added to the meal. "That was incredibly generous for them to give us dinner," I say, well aware that it costs half of their average day's wages for just the soda.

"To slaughter one of their livestock is a big gesture, but the people here like to express their appreciation," the minister says. "Too bad they don't have an air conditioning unit," he jokes. "Tonight's a hot one, even for me." Because of the heat, everyone keeps comfortable in either tank tops or Hawaiian t-shirts. It's Ok to wear these, now, because we are in the privacy of our own quarters. We dress more formally when we are in the village so we don't offend anyone.

I prepare lamb chops and potatoes with recently boiled water and add them to our meal as the main course. The table, which is really two smaller tables pushed together to fit the nine of us, is already set with purple, straw placemats and ivory colored candles. The candles are lit, the locally grown veggies and bread made from hand-milled flour are out, and now the coconut milk that the minister brought over is being poured. Soft drinks will be our dessert. As dinner gets underway conversation veers from past trips to the type of impact we are making on this current one.

"Well, we are almost done with the school's construction, but we didn't bring enough medical supplies again," Ed, one of the other missionaries, says. "We need more hypodermic needles, more pumps and more cleaning supplies."

"I still can't believe the sanitation here," Monica, a volunteer nurse who is more qualified than the local doctor, says. "I'm reusing swabs and scalpels. It's awful."

"It's rudimentary, but it's a start," Ed says referring to the one story, one roomed hospital.

"That's right," the minister affirms invoking positive chatter.

"Hear that," someone says.

"Well, clearly the school and hospital are a necessary start, but what else are we doing?" Lisa, another of the missionaries, asks quieting the chatter. Her passion begins to overtake her, "I mean, I see bits of western influence here and there, but their way of life is hierarchal and almost backwards compared to ours."

Many of the local people of Iambi and other parts of Tanzania live in fairly modern homes like the one we are in now and they have construction or administrative types of jobs. Often a family will have a cell phone or an outdated television hooked up to an oversized satellite dish. Both are justification for immense pride. But, most of the locals, the Masai people, are nomadic.

They live off of the land. They live in giant beehive looking mud huts, built by the women, which are composed of mud and different grasses. Hierarchical in society, the women are also in charge of gardening and washing. The washing is done against rocks and then hung to dry. The men are in charge of farming and hunting. Most of the families and tribes believe in a coming of age ceremony where a boy at 17 must venture out and spear a lion to death in order to become a man. And depending on the seasons, the rains, or flooding, a family or tribe will simply move to another spot and build another hut and create another farm.

"I just want to know that we are making a difference," Lisa follows up.

"Well, the electricity here is so minimal that I can barely charge my camera, so I'm definitely not going to say things are completely modern here," Dan says. He momentarily pauses before saying, "But the people here are some of the nicest people I've ever met. And they seem happy. I don't exactly think we should be trying to change their way of life. The greatest impact we can make is interaction."

"Go on," the minister says speaking for the whole table wanting to hear more.

"Well, as I've been taking snapshots and as Tom and I have been doing some filming; and Tom correct me if I'm wrong here, but I'm finding that they love the attention. They love that we care. It seems congruent with the human condition anywhere."

"Sounds right on," Tom says.

Now, I start to feel my passion take control of me, the connection that I often write about in my church devotionals. "I think it's important that we put that mutual attention to good use, to take that opportunity to spread the Word of the Lord," I say. The thought to me of someone facing death and not having Jesus by their side is terrifying. The thought tears me apart. I can't imagine anyone not being saved. "God says everyone will have the opportunity to hear the gospel and I would hate to think that it was my fault for not spreading the message."

"Now don't be taking my job," the local minister jokes.

"Come on guys, I think survival is always going to be the main religion here. Terrible things still happen like rapes, violence," Dan austerely adds. "We've all learned how severe the crime is here."

"Yeah that's right," Lisa says.

"Well…" I start to justify my argument, but the minister speaks up again in his deep, preacher voice.

"It's both, my friends," he says. We must help with both the positive things and the negative."

The night is incredibly hot and humid. It almost makes showering seem pointless because I'll be sweating until morning. The mosquitoes here carry malaria so we have to sleep with nets around the beds and they constantly drape on our faces. Dan probably finds it claustrophobic. We are both becoming insomniacs, but we rest as much as possible excited about our day tomorrow. After work, we are taking a long awaited safari.

TRANSCENDENCE - - - - Dan AGED 61 - - - - 2008

The two black Land Rovers are out of shape, outdated and probably wouldn't meet US specifications, but they do their job well in getting us up the Tanzanian mountain and into its massive crater. The crater, roughly five miles in diameter, is lush with jungle all around the edges and opens up to widespread plains, tall grasses, random patches of trees, scattered bodies of water, and hundreds of thousands of wild animals - basically, the bush. I'm elated because this present adventure is a life-long dream that has come true.

Roving through the lively jungle, our way to the bush is animated with birds, monkeys and gorillas dwelling behind a tangled maze of floral ornamented vines. Their chatter and howls can be heard from up in the trees as well. Babies ride on the backs of their mommas or cling to their bellies as they walk and climb. Spiders string long webs in open spaces.

Butterflies mix in with the flowers. Giraffes feed on the leafy under branches of high trees on the outskirts of the jungle leading into a rhino roaming, wildebeest herding preserve.

The breathtaking panorama makes me want to spend days here. There is so much to take in. Really, I could spend weeks here - what a kick for the National Geographic's photographers who set up camp in similar environments for weeks at a time studying animals in their natural habitat, watching them survive, waiting for the perfect shots.

As we begin our safari I wonder how much justice I will do the environment by taking photos from the vehicle and hanging onto the roll bars to steady myself. I don't have top flight equipment here and we're not setting up an encampment. Regardless, I'm thrilled with what I've got. Plus you never know when opportunity will strike.

Our driver guides us through the terrain, with a rifleman on his right side riding shotgun, my crew and I in the back seats scavenger hunting, not just for animals on this wild zoo tour, but for personality among the animals. Laurie and Brandon ride along in the car behind us with another driver and shooter. We roam slower than a golf cart, finding hippos swimming in swampy ponds, zebras rolling around like puppies, gazelle, hyenas, prairie dogs… Too many to possibly photograph them all. Screw weeks; I could spend a year here.

After driving for many hours in the sun, my adrenaline is still running, but running low. Most of the others are getting tired and hot. We approach a small forest of trees, which seem to have sprouted up in the middle of nowhere. The cooling shade brings a collaborative sigh of relief. Most of our travelers, even our riflemen, slouch back into their seats to refresh. Still standing, hanging onto the roll bars, I yell "stop".

Both vehicles stop and everyone sees what I'm looking at, an enormous elephant just twenty paces away. My heart pounds. This elephant could charge and turn our car over in a flash. But I seem to have this kinship with it and now I see it has a baby with her peering out from behind her legs. "Come on, give me a story," I mutter under my breath, looking through my camera lens ready to click snap. Snap. Snap. Snap. Snap. "Yes!"

We leave the outcropping of trees with collectively raised energies that will surely last us for the duration of our savanna driving. There are hundreds and hundreds of acres that we won't be able to touch because of time, but finding so many animals clustered together according to their herds and continually finding new animals keeps us positive. We are driving into knee high grass so there is no telling what we will find, but we keep our eyes peeled.

The drivers stop once again as we come across eight lions, a full grown male, two females, a couple adolescents and a few cubs, resting on a grassy mound. Animals instinctively go after people when they are hungry, but these lions apparently eat well because they unthreateningly take nominal interest in us. Instead they lounge, lazily flipping their tales at the flies. Still, I know there is a photo opp. When my camera beeps though, a flashing battery logo indicates low battery. After rummaging around my camera bag for the backup batter, I look up and see Brandon standing among the lions.

My jaw drops. The camera falls to the seat. I want to yell, but I don't want to spook the lions and cause a reaction. What is he doing? Our driver puts a finger in front of his lips and shushes the car. The shooter has his rifle up, locked against his shoulder and cheek, aimed at the lions. I don't think he'll be able to take them all out before one could thump Brandon. I turn back and look at the Land Rover behind us. The other shooter has his rifle aimed at the lions as well. I can tell Laurie is about to come undone, but their driver also shushes them. How could she let him out of the car? Why didn't anyone see or stop him?

Brandon lets out a deep, forced exhale, facing the lion pride. All of the lions, even the cubs, immediately stand and stare at Brandon. The hair on the back of my neck stands in the same fashion. They could eat him! The male, on all four legs, is as tall as Brandon's chin and his head is the size of Brandon's torso. I shoot looks at both of our riflemen who have now stiffened even more with fingers waiting and ready on the triggers, but still they don't fire. Why don't they fire? "Shoot," I insistently whisper. "Shoot."

Our driver shushes me again. "That's my son," I whisper back. He shushes me louder. *What do I do?* Then Brandon lets out a heavy growl. Astoundingly, seven of the eight lions simultaneously turn in the opposite direction and walk away. That's a relief, somewhat. I swear they would have attacked, but they're walking away. Still, one lion remains.

It's a female lion. Brandon and she stand toe to toe, face to face. Did the other lions leave so this one could finish him on her own? Surely the shooters can fire now. Why don't they fire?

None of us can take our eyes off of Brandon and the lion. Five long seconds of worry and amazement pass with Brandon and the lion looking at each other. They actually look at each other favorably. It's like they are having small talk, but Brandon being Dr. Doolittle is not a theory I want to test, especially not with a lion as a participant in this experiment. I can't believe this is happening.

Five more seconds pass and the lion looks past Brandon straight at me. Maybe she's looking at all of us, but it feels like she's giving me eye contact. What is happening? Then the lion turns and walks away after her pride. Brandon stands there for a moment and then returns to his seat in Laurie's Land Rover without saying a word. He has a tear running down his cheek.

"Brandon," I shout, as I questioningly look at him.

No response. I glance at Laurie and she raises her eyebrows, flabbergasted.

"He's crying," she mouths. I put my hands up in response more confused. Brandon sits next to Laurie, stares ahead and says nothing. I see their driver and their shooter look at each other like they are also confused. Then our driver says something in Swahili to our shooter.

We stay parked for several more minutes, but nothing happens. "Lion boy," our driver says looking at me in the rearview mirror. I give him an expression that shows I have no idea. "Let's go, I guess," I say. He starts the car and we all head out, at this point, certainly willing to end the tour.

TRANSCENDENCE - - - - Brandon AGED 23 - - - - 2008

It's as if I'd never heard the sound of the door close shut at our Campus View apartment. Normally there's too much commotion. Tim, Rob, Joel and I are always in a hurry, rushing in and out for class, practice, weight training, and airport runs. On the weekends when we're all home, there are always college parties. That's the college tennis life - nonstop commotion. The door was merely a thoughtless obstacle on the pathway to and from the bedrooms. It seemed an ambiguous detail before.

I heard the door close this time, though; the crisp seal, making the blue door flush with the poster lined wall. It knocked the winter wind back outside and knocked me stumbling inside onto the couch. This time, the closing of the door held significance. She left.

It's over. Regret. Staring at the gold peephole on the door, wondering where I went wrong, what I could have done differently, I try to relive the fond moments, but all I can do is think of the screw-ups.

There was the time we walked from her sorority and she slipped on an ice patch and fell. People across the street laughed and all I could do was laugh too.

There was the time I threw her ice cream cone in the trash and told her she didn't need it. "Why did I do that?" I berated myself, "projecting my own diet on her? She can have all the ice cream she wants."

And there was always my tennis traveling. If we ever had a fight beforehand, it was like a mini break up. I never made the time to call her during trips because I wanted to focus on my matches. Honestly, I was just glad to be focusing at all. Of course, I couldn't tell her that.

She made up in her mind that I wouldn't always be there for her, understandably. It's not like I was a pillar of support. All the time exceedingly passionate, either adoring or quarrelsome, I had fought for us before, several times actually. I wanted to be there for her and I told myself that constantly. Tennis, what helped me to focus, had become too much of a priority.

My eyes watering, I can't believe this. "That was love." The thought struck me as though new. I'd never before been able to handle that, not for myself, or another.

I realize how much I truly care for her. Tears trickle down my face. That was love and now it's gone. I would have gladly given up tennis for that. I would have worked at a gas station and lived in a hut on the side of a mountain - anything for that girl.

The great thing about her is that she would never ask me to give up on what my dreams told me to do.

"My dreams, my stupid dreams!"

Tauntings are what they are. Whatever inspiration, whatever pro aspiration they try to instill, it's just not worth it.

Classic rackets hang on the walls between some of the posters. Two of my current rackets are on the couch next to me.

"No, no, I just don't see the point."

Then, in need of escapism, I stand up and rip off my tennis clothes. I angrily strip nude. Then I scoop up my own rackets and yank the other rackets from the walls, and tear the damn door open, and march outside. I march down the three flights of steps to the parking lot and heave the rackets in a pile on the ground.

One by one, I smash the rackets into the ground, trying to hack craters out of the concrete. Yelling nonsense, almost screaming hysterically, I crack a racket and fling it, not caring where it may land. Then I grab another, and another.

"Fuck tennis!" Crack!

"Fuck school!" Crack!

"And fuck!" Crack! "Just fuck!"

"I hate all this shit!" Crack! "ROOAAAHHHHHR," I let out a lion's roar.

Then with no more rackets to destroy, I stand tall and find neighbors from all three apartment levels gathered on their balconies staring at me in shock. Breathing heavily, "Feel my wrath," I feel like shouting at them. Instead, I walk back up to my unit.

During my naked walk upstairs, there's this feeling of emptiness, like a bad stomach ache. I can see how depression's sway could cause a person to jump off of a bridge and land flat as a pancake, or even a three story balcony, if only it were higher. I'm dying in so many of these dreams anyways. Why not the real thing? It would even be simple to get hold of a gun and pull the trigger - a brain splattering shot. But depression doesn't have that suicidal sway over me. That's too crazy, even for me.

The empty, stomach ache feeling is sharp as a knife and as much as I can't bear it, I like it. It's awakening.

I can let go. Tennis, school, life, I can let it all go.

"No, I don't want to end things."

Instead, why not take the time to just let myself actually be crazy. No more fighting against it.

If I'm crazy, let it be.

Feeling racy, it's time to let loose - impulsively buy extravagant things, steal a fast car and drive recklessly, gamble, drink, smoke, party, play with women until we're exhausted, and then sleep with the lot - I should take the time, as mother would say, to sin.

"That sounds alright actually. Fuck school. I'm going to Vegas, tonight."

~ ~ ~

CHAPTER 15IFTEEN

TRANSCENDENCE - - - - Chelsea AGED 21 - - - - 2008

OK, the main character here is Chidi, an African tribal boy who loses his younger brother to a hijacking gang. *Interesting*. And when a traveling missionary teaches Chidi about Psalms 91, an empowering prayer from the Bible, he finds himself inspired to rescue his brother. He surmounts to dangerous obstacles along the way, of course, one of which is a pride of lions.

When the missionary tells Chidi about Psalms 91, she quotes the first line, "He that dwelleth in the secret place of the most high shall abide under the shadow of the Almighty," and explains her understanding of the prayer that the secret place is consciousness - that God must be contacted from within and from there he offers his protection. The word 'consciousness' snags my attention as I look at the giant dry erase board on the neighboring wall next to my desk.

My room, which I consider my live-in think tank, is a sanctuary for sleep, research and homework. Two of Dad's photographs hang on adjacent walls, while the other two walls are dedicated to theories about Brandon - mounted on one wall is a giant dry erase board with a new hypothesis every month. Mounted above my desk on the other wall is a giant corkboard with pinned articles as well as my own notes.

On the dry erase board, I've most recently drawn an outlined head and shoulders silhouette of a man. Inside the head I've drawn a pie chart labeling different functions of the mind, PERSONALITY, EGO, CONSCIOUS, SUBCONSCIOUS, ANALECT, MEMORIES, PERCEPTIONS, IMAGINATION. Sometimes I string the concepts together in different orders trying to come up with possible scenarios that Brandon could be dealing with.

Often I'll come up with something that goes like this: Brandon consciously told himself to go to a subconscious place where he takes on his preferred personality. He did that and now he's stuck there and waking from such a place would be like the opposite of telling yourself to go to sleep. I guess he would have to first realize he was in that place. Then the thought occurs to me. "He could have found unaccounted traits that he didn't know he developed or traits that he didn't expect."

It's frustrating because I don't really know. I just think of these confusing concepts that lead nowhere and are impossible to prove. I'll even further my concepts and think maybe he created a dream-like place beyond his analytical mind. Maybe in that place he has the skill set and personality to be nearly perfect and doesn't want to leave it. I don't know. I can't stop theorizing. It's become a habit.

'Habit vs. Instinct' is on one of the notes written on my corkboard. I have 'perspective' written on there as well. It seems all I do is come up with this stuff. I honestly wish I would stop thinking of these things and just accomplish something of value.

The missionary quotes another line from Psalms 91, "Thou shalt tread upon the lion," and the missionary says that the lion stands for difficulty about which we know. "Amazing, they go to Africa, but come away stimulated by Brando," I think to myself, referring to Mom's and Dad's missionary trip. "And who would have thought I would be the first one to miss out on a family vacation? I don't know if I can take this."

Feeling overwhelmed, I take a deep breath and look around the room. My bed, a nightstand, a trunk at the foot of the bed and my desk are the only things I allow on the floor. The room never changes and I never allow a mess, so when I look around the room, it's not to inspect for changes, but more to keep me in the moment.

My desk, which is constructed out of metal tubing and smooth wood, painted a polished black, is more like a modern work station instead of a desk. It has seven open shelves built in on the right side going from the floor up. Some of the shelves are dedicated to classes, some are for Brandon, and some are for both. In printed labels from top to bottom they read: GERONTOLOGY, PSYCHOLOGY, HUMAN SCIENCE, SUBCONSCIOUS, PRE-MED, THEORIES, and RESEARCH. I don't need shelves for the easy subjects. The sleek style and functionality of the whole unit usually helps me feel organized, especially when I'm besieged with assignments, research and miscellaneous stuff like editing Mother's church play as I'm doing for her now.

"Uh, I can't do this. I have too much on my plate right now. I told Mom I would though. What should I do? Ok, let me look at my schedule and see where my priorities are," I think as I pick up the notebook planner from the left side of my desk, to the left of my laptop.

My notebook planner has '*find a solution*' which I write at the top of every week giving myself orders for Brandon. So far at the end of every week I've been replying, "I wish-"

"Mom's play, OK, see I've got no time for this," I say overlooking my collaborative assignments. "See I've got, well, maybe if I rearrange…" I redo my calendar three times before I realize I'm procrastinating on everything instead of actually tackling anything. A panic starts to rise because I hate wasting time. I don't want to sacrifice my whole life on this bullshit.

"How am I the first one to miss a family vacation?" I think again. "It's the one thing that keeps us normal. I'm the one who is trying to find a solution to make Brandon normal. Talk of crazy, I think I'm going crazy."

I stand up from my desk and curl into bed. Never have I felt lonelier.

TRANSCENDENCE - - - - Brandon AGED 24 - - - - 2009

Sophie answers the knock at the door with a natural poise. Who could it be? She slowly, gently pulls the door partway open revealing eighty percent of her slender stature to whoever just knocked. For a couple of seconds she stands there in her pink and black lingerie looking at the man who knocked and she says nothing. She's almost looking at the man from her peripheral vision because she is also gazing out to see if anyone else is coming.

When she realizes it's just this shaggy haired man dressed in jeans and an Ed Hardy t-shirt, - (what a cliché!) - she leans her body weight forward resting her right shoulder on the edge of the door and languidly queries in a long, drawn out French accent, "yes?"

The man almost stutters, but then remembers he had every right to be there. He quickly pulls himself together and then confidently chuckles, "Hi, I'm Nick from City Lights Magazine. Is Brando here? We have an interview scheduled for this time."

Unhappy with the evident identity of her new company, she overtly rolls her eyes. Then as if her demeanor wasn't intimidating enough, she walks away, back into the hotel suite, leaving Nick hanging in the doorway.

"Hi, Nick is it?" I ask throwing a jacket over my Ralph Lauren pajamas. I hurry to greet him.

"Yes, Nick. Wow, Mr. Under Cover Vegas - discovered, very cool. It's nice to meet you," he says extending his hand. "Is this still a good time?"

"Yep, now is great. I just uh… Let's not do the interview here. Do you mind if we do it at the roulette table?"

Nick briefly pauses because he's never done an interview at a roulette table, but then gives a certain look at the hotel room in silent appraisal. He seems to understand that I want to give Sophie space to freshen up. "Yeah, that's easy," he says.

"Great. Let's walk. Sophie told me about a betting strategy, the Martingale strategy, and I want to try it out."

"Was that Sophie?" Nick asks.

"Yeah that was Sophie."

"I see you live up to your reputation."

Ignoring the implication, "Yeah anyways, she's from France and she was rapping about roulette and a winning strategy. She said it's a French game from the 18th century. I said, but you're not from the 18th century. She said her relatives were. I didn't get into it any further with her, but I'll give the strategy a shot."

"Ok, cool. Let's see how you go. I'll just throw out questions here and there while we cruise. Can we start now?" he asks as we enter the elevator.

"Fire away," I say, and tap the 'casino' button.

As the elevator swoops down Nick states his first official question, "How did you come to Vegas?"

Before I answer I gaze through the glass walls of the elevator and survey the Luxor's inner workings. Recalling how I made this hollowed out replica pyramid of a hotel my home, I gander over a smorgasbord of entertainment venues - the hotel concierge ready to check guests in or grant any requested desire (for a price of course), the casino floor with slot machines and table games, the poker room, and off to the sides near the slanted walls are entrances to the LAX night club, restaurants, the buffet, the pool area, theaters, private wings and other galleries. All of it is Egyptian in theme and I make use of all of it as if it is the family room in my own house. I use any and all of the amenities as I please. The hotel guests are like my guests. I talk to whomever I please.

"I came here just recently really - about eight months ago. I was in college when something mentally went off and I just didn't see any point in finishing. I was an athlete on the tennis team there. With that and an extra load of classes and a girlfriend it was overload. It was work instead of play. Life wasn't good. So one night I bought a plane ticket and I flew to Vegas. I flew here and now I do whatever I want. I Play."

Nick gives me a nodding smile and says, "That's pretty good. Most people don't do whatever they want."

"If only, right?"

"I don't think most would be successful," Nick replies.

"Maybe I'm just lucky then. Good timing," I say as we step out of the elevator. I know the layout of the gaming floor like I know home back in Portland so I lead as Nick follows me through the busyness. As we walk he asks, "But how did you start making money with that approach - just playing?"

I speak over slot machine tunes. "Mm, to be honest I was more than overworked at the end of my college term. I was very depressed and when I first came here I was still lingering in that depression's aftermath. Making money wasn't on the top of my list of things to do. If I had to live off credit cards, I wasn't concerned. I didn't have a backup plan. I just needed to free up. I needed to be free."

I feel good now, but I still get a random stomach ache that I got from the bad living. It keeps me awake at times. But as a result, I stay more awake than most. I keep talking as we arrive at the roulette tables. I select one with the fewest participants and put down two g's.

"Fortunately, I never had to worry about it. I started playing poker and I doing well at it."

"So do you consider yourself a poker pro?" Nick follows.

"Oh not really, I make most of my money at other stuff. I just find poker to be very similar to tennis. Once you get down to a heads up situation, you just need a slight advantage to win. Plus, sometimes, I can get into this certain mental zone state. It helps me perform well."

"Interesting," Nick says. "I get that."

"Yeah I think so. Hey, did you know roulette is French for small wheel," I say as the croupier, the roulette dealer, slides stacks of white chips across the felt in front of me.

"No I didn't know that," Nick says, looking at the red and black spinning wheel. Ready to throw down my first bet, I touch the chips, but out of nowhere a vision slaps me like a seizure.

"So how does this Martingale strategy work," I hear Nick ask, but his voice is distant. I'm too far gone to respond. I'm in a different place. It's an older time.

I hold my gloved hand out allowing the driver to help me balance as I step down to the cobble stone ground from the carriage. One of several horses tied to the hitching posts softly neighs. I see her and then look back feeling proud of the two beautiful beasts that pulled my carriage, surely thoroughbreds. I glance back to the driver who just released my hand after ensuring my safety to the ground. He bows his head. I curtsey. "Thank you for the ride," I say, placing a franc in his hand.

He bows his head again. "Enjoy the evening Madame."

In silk, strappy heels I drift up the steps and onto the foyer esplanade, making my entrance at the Casino de Paris. The casino is full of activity, but people stop and stare. Oh how people stare.

I often draw stares, but tonight they look at me as if I'm Queen Marie. Ladies stare the most. Waving fans upon their faces, they stare on. Even the wallpaper stares.

It's not my new, sleeveless, low-necked robe. This is just a gown. I hold their stares because I'm glowing with a brand new fashion they've never seen - my hair.

Most ladies, holding their heads very still right now, steady powdered wigs taller than high hats. Their styles are accentuated with died shades of pastel blues, pinks or purples and adorned with feathers or ribbons or tassels or lace. It's a garden full of Easter eggs.

I however, have gone natural. My hair is a mass of beautiful curls - simple as that. I feel light. I feel cute. I'm free as a girl, here to play a game in the garden, roulette. It's another wheel game, but it's the latest enchantment.

I swan over to a table full of suited gentlemen and wigged ladies. They immediately part, to create a space for the duchess - me.

"Welcome to the table Madame," the banker says. I smile and greet everyone at the table.

"Credit, please," I say to the banker. "Whatever you think is appropriate."

He guesses and places an average sized stack of white painted, wooden chips in front of me on the round table. Looking at the grooved 'E','O' betting pockets around the wheel, I think this won't be enough. "More please," I say, raising a few more eyebrows around the table. No one however, is too surprised as the banker slides two more stacks in front of me. I give him an equal amount of francs in return and then pick up one chip, ready to place my first bet.

As I do though, the table changes from a round stonework table with a spinning 'E','O' wheel in the center to a lined and numbered, green, felt topped, racetrack-shaped table with a spinning red and black wheel on the edge. The wooden chips transform to plastic. People, instead of garbed in formal wear are either more casual or more promiscuous in dress. Many of the dudes around the tables are sporting dress shirts and jeans; either that or V-necks or hooded sweaters. Many of the chicks are all but popping out of strapless boob tube tops or skimpy little dresses that look like they should be t-shirts.

Somewhat thrown off by the French vision, I try to grasp reality. *It's been a while since that happened.* Nick, with sunglasses on top of his head holding his shaggy hair back, is awaiting a response.

"Sorry, what were you asking me?" I mumble.

"I was asking about your strategy," Nick says earnestly.

"My strategy," I repeat to myself trying to play it cool. I can't help, but conclude that Sophie heavily promoting the Martingale strategy influenced my recent vision of the duchess. "Play it cool, B," I warn myself and aloud, - "Right, well I'm going to place a minimum bet on black. If I win, then I will continue to make minimum bets on black earning a small, steady profit. If I lose…" As soon as I grab a white chip and drop it on black the environment changes again from 2009 Las Vegas back to the 18th century Rococo period in France.

I like watching the little wheel spin round. It's mesmerizing! In fact, it must have caused me to zone out and dither away my opportunity to bet because the banker asks, "Madame, have you played this game before?" The table looks at me as though I may be helpless. "It's quite new and I'd be happy to…"

Well, we can't have the table thinking that. "No, no, I've not played before, but I have no doubt it is uncomplicated. I've heard of it. I've heard it's new. I've also heard about a winning strategy."

"Really?" a gentleman in a well groomed, white mustache inquires. "If you don't mind my asking, what do you mean?"

I briefly look at the people around the table and then at the gentleman who poses the question. Giving my lopsided half smile, "I am no gambler".

"You're not gambling?" the gentleman understandably questions.

"No, I'm not gambling, not at all. I'm not here to play 'Roly Poly' or the 'Poker'. I simply want an evening at the casino with you fine people," I answer causing some of the party to smile at the thought of being considered by me. "But why would I just gamble money away when I could play profitably? That's right - play profitably. Would anyone like to hear my strategy?"

"Please," the gentleman answers as he, and the banker, and the rest of the table listens intently.

"Now I presume the 'E' betting pocket in front of me stands for 'even' and the 'O' pocket stands for odd," I say giving the banker deliberate eye contact.

"That is correct Madame and the double zero…"
Some of the table giggles at this obvious observation.

I interrupt, "And so I will start a small bet on, let's say, 'Even'. If the tiny ball lands on any 'Even' number 2-24 I shall double my money. This is obvious because these are the rules of the game. However, my tactics come into play when I lose. Do you see how I have more than an average amount of chips in front of me? It's not because of my greed, no. It's because if I lose on an 'Even' bet I shall double my bet on 'Even' again, and double again, and again, until the tiny ball does land on an 'Even' number and I recover all of my original losses. If the tiny ball lands in a double zero, which I presume is the casino's pocket…"

"That is correct Madame," the banker quietly affirms.

"Then, I shall consider it the same as if the tiny ball landed on an odd number and I shall double my bet on 'Even' yet again. Now, everyone may feel free to watch as I test out the betting system. Shall we begin?"

I place a bet on 'Even' as I said I would and the banker rolls the tiny ball and spins the wheel. I love watching the wheel speed up and then gradually slow to a stop.

"Eight," the banker announces giving me my first win and a small applause from the table members. Silly really, I didn't do much to earn their kinship, but a win still feels good.

In the moment of their applause, the scene changes back to Vegas. Instead of illustrations of dainty women and cigarette ads hanging on the wallpapered walls, lit-up, bigger-than-life-sized images of Chris Angel, Carrot Top and the latest porn stars now adorn the walls. And instead of two violinists playing melodies in the corner, the music changes to electronic tunes from the nearby slot machines and pop beats coming out of the Luxor speakers.

Again I'm thrown off, but I find myself recuperating easier from the reoccurring French vision than the first time. *It's not like I don't have experience with this shit. Maybe, I'll never be free. Oh well. What will be, will be.*

The minimum bet I placed on black lost so I place another bet on black, but this time doubled. The ball rolls around the spinning wheel and lands on a red number. I lose again, and the croupier sweeps my betted chips away. I double down, again, and lose, again. It's been red three times in a row.

Having started with a ten dollar bet, I find myself putting eighty dollars worth of chips on black after the cold streak. It's bound to be black this time.

"Ah, another question," Nick says sees I'm not having fun losing. "I've heard rumors - several different versions - of how you came to be known as this Under Cover Vegas identity, especially in such a short amount of time. And I don't mean to be ignorant, but I have to admit, I hadn't heard of you before my editor assigned the story. Would you enlighten me?"

People around the table now look at me, wondering who I am and why I'm being interviewed. Tourists don't know me. Most local residents don't know me for that matter. "Yeah, that's cool. Since I initially started living off of poker, I just lived in the casino hotel, here at the Luxor. And since it became my home, I started walking around in jammies and a suite jacket. If I was going to feel free, I was going to be comfortable too."

"I notice the outfit now," Nick mentions.

"Yeah, and you know I'm not sure how a reputation came out of all of it. I wasn't looking for popularity. What escalated the narrative is that I wore the same outfit to the nightclubs. Obviously, I knew about their strict dress codes, but I also knew celebrities didn't have to follow them, so someone must be loosening policy. One night I walked past a line where the wait looked like it would have been more than an hour. I went up to the bouncer, put five hundred bucks in his hand, and he let me straight in. The cash was no sweat off my back since I was going well at cards. To him, I was just one dude to overlook. Since it worked, I did it more, and then all the time, at any club. They must have spread word because after a couple weeks many bouncers didn't just overlook me, they started looking for me. They'd give me nods as I approached, spotting my pajama dress. They let me in before chicks. They let me in faster than they did some celebs."

Nick and much of the table stare at me, listening, "Then one day when I was playing poker at the Wynne, a lady named Debra, introduced herself as an agent, and said she'd heard of me. She said I was like an underwear renegade because of the jammies. Pretty soon she got me a few gigs doing some modeling. Whatever the brand, it was good money."

"Now, instead of bribing bouncers, I get paid to show up to clubs. Whatever club wants me, wearing jammies and a jacket, both arms full of models; I walk past the lines like I'm baby Hughie. I'm no celeb, but the manager over at the Moon nightclub told me I created a momentary desire for the dudes who wait in line, making them more anxious to get in. And for me, when I get in, everything is VIP bottle service - thousand dollar Dom Perignon. I don't pay for shit. But I still throw a tip to some of the bouncers."

"And you live in a suite now," Nick asks.

"Yeah, the Luxor upgraded me to a suite, complimentary. They send me fruit baskets and tickets to shows."

"Wow, so Mr. Under Cover Vegas…," Nick elongates waiting for me to finish his sentence.

"Yeah, well, I guess it's behind the scenes stuff. I don't know. I didn't come up with it. Don't ask me. Ask your editor."

Nick states another question as I continue losing and doubling down more bets on black. "You must like where you've come thus far, but what direction do you see yourself going next?"

"I don't know to be honest. The whole experience is surreal. It's been sweet, but it actually is like a dream." That thought has me pause for a second, considering my crazy mind. *Oh well, what will be, will be.*

The croupier sweeps more of my chips away as I double down again, betting $640. Then the scene changes back to the Casino de Paris.

After the table applause I place another small wager on 'Even', but the tiny ball falls on nine. It's so close to the last number, eight. "Ok, time to shine," I say as I place twice the amount of chips into the 'Even' betting square. The banker rolls the ball around the spinning wheel, but when it comes to rest in an odd numbered pocket I find myself ruffled.

"Double it again," I say putting more chips in the betting square, hoping to hit 'Even' this time. The tiny ball spins round and dies on thirteen. One lady whispers to her husband. I feel like I'm not backing up my word. This system is meant to be a coin flip, but I've seen loss and loss. How unlucky.

I double the amount again, and again, I encounter another loss. A few more bets at this rate and I won't be able to endure the loss. I'm going to be the first one out and I started with the most. I should have purchased more chips. How can the tiny ball always land odd? This is a devilish game.

"Money doubles fast in this game, but I shall have another go," I say wondering where the evil ball is going to rest. Some of the table looks worried.

"Twenty," the banker announces giving me a win large enough to cover my previous losses and a small profit. The table claps in support.

Happy with my minor accomplishment in proving my system, I inform the table, "I shall retire now. Thank you for your company." The room brightens as the chandelier lighting morphs to Luxor lighting.

New York, Miami and Las Vegas are considered America's sleepless cities. Staying awake in Vegas is usually easy, but these dreams have me questioning myself, and in the midst of a stupor. I'm still losing. If I'm forced to double my bet even once more I will be over the table limit. Technically this is my last bet. It's about two grand and I can cop the loss, but I'd rather not.

"This Martingale system has me feeling shaky," I proclaim as the ball travels around the spinning wheel. *Come on. She won*, I think, referring to the duchess. *Let me win.* It makes three laps, and four, and five, and six, and slows touching down in zero's pocket, but rolls more and settles on 32 red.

"Oh, that's weak," Nick says coming to my aid.

The table knows I can't double down again, and surprisingly, they seem sorry for me. I don't want to give them a reason to feel sorry, and I don't feel sorry for myself, but part of me does. My competitive side just hates losing at anything. *Well, let it go, Brando.*

Stepping away from the table, "Hey Nick, let's finish this another time, eh? I'm going to go check on Sophie."

We go in separate directions.

I don't head for Sophie. I shoot her a text: GONNA PLAY POKER. LET'S MEET UP LATER. I head outside and hail a cab.

The cabbie drives North on Las Vegas Boulevard driving me towards the Bellagio. Since dusk hunkers down on the city, I turn to see if the Luxor light is on. It is. The Luxor Light, a light that shoots upward from the tip of the pyramid, a light that Magician Chris Angel levitated over, is the brightest light in the world. Because of that beaming light, this pyramid is in the same prestigious category as the actual Egyptian pyramids, being a part of the seven manmade wonders of the world. Supposedly the light, along with the pyramids, can be seen from space with a naked eye.

Each time I pull away from the replica pyramid and sphinx, I find myself remembering our time in sandy Cairo as well as many other family travels. I miss the family, Mom and Dad and Chelsea and even Humphrey. I don't need my childhood though. Enough was enough. Besides, they want me to be free just as much as I want my freedom.

Without fail, I'm always quickly distracted from the Luxor's beam and the dismay of insistent family and personal memories by the rest of the strip's flashing lights. The lights can't be seen from space, but they have the radiance of a Christmas tree and I never tire of looking at them. They convey everything from gigantic lit up guitars and motorcycles to colored water shows and Caesar statues to a shimmering Eifel tower and more. The lights and sights are vastly different, but somehow flow together magnificently. They cured the depression I had when I first moved here.

When the driver drops me off at the Bellagio I'm thinking of another freedom move. On my way to the poker room, I stroll through my favorite lobby, which always looks like it's been designed by Edward Scissor-Hands - every week a new forest of animal shaped plants.

Along the way, assessing my evening plans, I pass Michael Jordan who will probably wind up at his favorite nightclub here, The Bank. I've seen him in the VIP section there a few times. He looks at me like he vaguely recognizes me, but he recognizes me because of the Polo pajama outfit I'm wearing. I can tell he sort of wonders who I am. I give him a trivial nod, thinking keep on moving Mike; you're the real deal, unlike my fake ass. We go on about our separate business.

Had I been the little boy I once was I would have found motivation in Jordan's presence alone. Seeing him now though, is seeing another man who tackled his life's calling which only points out that I haven't done much of anything. The combination of the French vision, losing at roulette, Nick's question about my life's direction, and seeing Jordan, turns my mood sour. Outside of the poker room I follow through with my planned stop to the cashier's cage - I ask for three hundred and fifty grand.

It's a heap of money, but it only takes a minute for them to transfer it from my Luxor account, where I keep my bankroll. I've got some additional savings and more money due to me from recent gigs, but this is pretty much it. The last time I played with all of my cash, it was much less and I was on my Kamikaze run as a lucky Vegas rookie.

I guess I still am a rookie because if I wasn't I might not be making this withdrawal. But fuck it. I'm not sure whose life I'm living anymore. Whether I'm trying to 'BE LIKE MIKE' or whether I'm living in the footsteps and visions of other people. Whatever! I need to live. I need to *fully* live.

Nine players, including myself, are seated at a No-Limit cash game in the Bellagio's high stakes poker room. I start profiling the other players right away.

From the dealer's left:

Two clean-shaven, balding, fat fellas, both wearing collared golf shirts - one shirt maroon, the other, navy blue pin stripes over white. They must be pals or wealthy business partners or perhaps both.

Seated beside the two of them is an older lady who looks like she could be a country-western singer with short bleached blond hair pushed away from her face with Armani sunglasses.

Next is a shiny headed black dude in a white, Gucci dress shirt with a smile as big as Terrell Owens. Oh wait; it is Terrell Owens, another compadre who's trying to live. However, T.O. is worth close to $100 million from NFL contracts and other endorsements. That's real. That and I highly doubt if he's been through what I've been through.

Some guy wearing a curved ball cap, whiskery scruff on his face, and a white v-neck t-shirt is sitting next to T.O. What must be a 36 hour shadow and the darkness around his eyes gives the impression that his session is nearing an end. Impressively though, he has at least a million dollars in front of him.

To the right of the scruffy guy is a young brunette chick wearing a revealing caramel colored blouse.

After her, I notice is a want-to-be gagster; a clean shaven, white dude sporting a backwards cap and a Pistons jersey, both of which are too big for him. He's wearing a thick, gold bracelet - a tournament trophy, I realize with amusement.

Last is an Indian kid who looks younger than me, wearing a Harvard hooded sweatshirt.

I join them in my jacket and jammies.

Not long after I sit down, the country-singer lady (at least, that's who she is in my mind) goes bust and leaves the table. Her seat is filled with the next player on the waiting list, Tom Dwan. I've played with him before, at some smaller 2-5 tables. He's a year younger than me, but he's been an internet poker pro since he was 19. I think he's made $4 million on just tournament prize money. Who knows how much he's earned in cash games like these? He's certainly made more than me. I don't have *any* big wins.

The $350 thou that I'm sitting behind has me sitting average with the rest of the table, except of course, for the guy in the curved brimmed cap with over a million dollars in front of him. But the kicker is when Tom sits down he's sitting at a table full of peers, similarly wealthy people who can willingly buy back in at any point if they lose their chips. Or so it seems, but what's not common table knowledge is that *I* can't buy back in. I'm playing for all of my lute. With only one bullet in the chamber, I'm ready to ride or die.

An hour into play, I'm holding King Queen of clubs. The first fat guy limps, the second one folds. Tom limps and T.O. folds. A raise to $2,000, two callers, my call, and the limpers' follow-up calls gets us tantalizingly close to a family sized pot. Seven of us anticipate the dealt flop seeking a chance to win the $14,000 in the middle of this smoothly pelted poker table.

Only three of the other six players remaining in the hand are wearing their game faces. After playing against them for an hour though, this isn't exactly a cakewalk. Each one of these 'gamble-holic', 'mathlete' poker players plays better poker in their sleep than the majority of the people in the world do at their pinnacle. And until now, in challenging them, I would have thought my leverage against these guys was something similar to that of Patrick Antonius, who used tennis skills to become a poker super freak. But I'm not Patrick Antonius so my only leverage is my antagonistic temperament.

It's time to start zoning.

As the flop is flawlessly dealt over the Bellagio emblem in the center of the table, I'm staring at the other players. I'm reading their emotions - raised eyebrows, hand gestures, slumped shoulders, smirks, breathing patterns, everything. Before I even look at the flop, I want to determine who liked it and who didn't. Then I look at the flop and see if it helped my hand.

The flop: Ace of clubs, 7 of hearts, and 10 of diamonds. Fingers twitch. The brunette brushes a hand through her hair. A few exchanged looks orbit around the table. Some players hold perfectly still.

The second stage of betting: check, check, a bet of $8,000, call, call and then my turn. Shuffling my chips with my left hand, I carefully consider my situation. My tennis genes want me in a heads up situation. The odds are better when fighting one on one. I re-raise $20,000, raising the stakes higher, hoping to scare any or all people away.

The first fat guy doesn't seem to have liked the flop so he quickly folds. Tom considers calling, but surprisingly loses his nerve and folds. The scruffy dude in the brimmed cap, the original raiser, re-raises me to $55,000 to establish his seriousness. The move puts pressure on me because the pot is climbing quickly. All I have is a gut shot straight draw and he's playing like he has five aces. The two players between us call, each putting in $55,000. What are they calling with? There's well over $180,000 in the pot. Even if I had nothing, calling $35,000 more is a worthy investment. Besides, I could be holding six aces for all they know. I make an easy call.

The dealer lays out the turn card, the 7 of clubs. That puts two clubs on the board, giving me a one in four chance of hitting the nut flush on the river. Also, if I hit a Jack of any suit, I will have a Broadway straight.

Those are two good possibilities, but my intentions are to bully my way through this hand so I don't necessarily need to hit my cards. I've been playing a lot of hands in the past hour. Maybe they'll think I'm loose. Maybe they'll think I got lucky hitting a second seven on the turn. Acting the part, after the guy in the brimmed cap checks and two more checks, I bet sixty percent of the pot, building it to over $370,000. That's more than my current bankroll. This hand is either going to bankrupt me or double my wealth. The scruffy checker tags along. The other two fold.

We are down to heads up, but we are also down to just one card to come. The river is a Jack of spades. Nice, I've hit my straight. I've got to be sitting good now. If he checks though, I'll check back. This hand has been exciting enough. I don't want to put any unnecessary money in the pot, giving him a chance to come back over the top of me.

My current opponent, the guy in the brimmed cap with about a million dollars in front of him, shuts his eyes for a few seconds. I wonder if he's going to fall asleep. Then he opens his eyes as big as he can and bets $200,000 covering the rest of my chips, putting me all in. What?

Trying to work out what he has, I replay the hand in my head. He raised it pre-flop and re-raised on the flop, but then he slowed down on Fourth Street. Is he slow playing me? What could he have, Ace King, Ace Ten, Ace Jack? He wouldn't be playing with the third seven? Pocket sevens? That would be sick. My straight is nearly the best possible hand anyways.

Does he have pocket Aces, pocket Tens? Ooh that'd be a nasty full house. Maybe he has the same hand, King Queen. We would split the pot. I'd hate having to call just to split, but it's better than a major loss.

"Trying to scare me off?" I ask hoping for a reaction.

Nothing.

I grasp what I can of my short hair, tilt back and groan staring into a bright ceiling light.

*

RRROARR! (I see you, fire ball!)

The warmth feels erotic. I see you fire ball!

I nod, and then look across the land.

Staring into the sun has temporarily blinded me. I see a dark swarm of bees, shaped like another lion, yet covered in shadow. Who is that? Is that my lady lion?

"Let go," the shadow whispers, then vanishes.

*

The dry, grassy field turns to faux green felt.

The veteran dealer announces that it is my turn to act.

Another damn vision? I wonder how long I've been stagnant. I'd better make a play here.

Is he bluffing, thinking I won't risk the rest of my chips? Does he put me on my straight? Maybe he's been playing so long that his judgment is off.

Cloaked by a sleepy poker face, he's too hard to read. Is he patient, or just sleepy? I have no idea what to put him on.

I swear I was done with these visions?

Ok, Ok. I'm going to let fate provide the answer. If I call and I win, then I'm on the right track, poker and all. If I lose, if I go broke, then I go in a different direction.

I flip up my cards showing my straight to see if he reacts.

Nothing. Other eyes raise from other players.

"Call," I say, the statement giving me a reckless confidence. No one says a word. He looks at my flipped up cards a little surprised. Then he looks down at his own cards. He flips them to show me and the rest of the table.

"Four of a kind, Sevens," the dealer announces reading the cards for the man in the brimmed cap.

He had four of a kind - four of a kind? My stomach rises to my throat. Four of a kind is a monster.

He reaches his arms across the middle of the table and hugs the messy pile of chips pulling them close. Add it to his million plus.

My Vegas money - gone. My poker run - done. Mr. Under Cover has just unraveled. Vegas chewed him up and spit him out in one hand.

Voiceless, emotionless, I stand up from my seat and walk away.

~ ~ ~

CHAPTER 16IXTEEN

TRANSCENDENCE - - - - Brandon AGED 24 - - - - 2010

Glistening, golden splashes of water part from my board as I pick up enough speed to pop up and balance and then ride. I'm riding on top of the world. The dichotomy of moving with the wave is like the relationship between free will and divine plan. It's why locals call surfing the life.

Subliminally absorbing what makes Kailua beach a top ten beach of the world, my subconscious takes in the sun beams overhead, the smooth, sandy beach at water's edge, the multimillion dollar beach front properties including President Obama's holiday retreat house, swaying palm trees in between, and the island of Oahu behind. At the same time, my conscious is zoned into the breeze against my face and my balanced body sliding down the rolling wave, my speed building like a skateboard on a half pipe. It sends me on a rewarding dash.

After the wave dies down, wanting another ride, I paddle back out to the break, where the ocean floor drops off. On my way, another surfer pops up on a noticeably larger wave, giving us a show. "It's a perfect wave," I can't help but silently admire.

His bald head makes me think, "Slater." This guy looks nothing like pro surfer, Kelly Slater, but with his in-action aura outshining his own appearance, the two could be identical twins. His surfing is flawless as he moves laterally, carving. He sharply pivots up beyond the tip of the wave to catch air, spins 180 degrees and slides back down the face of the wave. I turtle dive under the wave as it passes and he cruises by, making the most of his ride. "Who was that?" I wonder. Inspired, I paddle more efficiently to get my next turn.

Though Kailua beach is beautiful, the waves come in dodging spurts. Sometimes it can be ten minutes before a good one comes. There are a dozen other individual surfers evenly spaced along the break, waiting for what could be a perfect curling wave as I join. It's an obvious, unwritten code, that unless we feel like chatting, we give each other plenty of space.

Like the other surfers, I straddle my board and wade my feet around in the water. Methodically bobbing up and down over the smaller waves, I look for signs of the ocean current heaving enough force into the drop-off wall below, to ensure that I'll be ready for the next perfect wave.

"Sweet day," I hear a calm voice say bringing my focus back above the ocean's surface. It's the bald surfer. His dark skin isn't from the sun and he's not Hawaiian. He looks Thai, I decide.

"Yeah it's good," I say. "Nice ride back there. I'm looking for a similar wave so I can do the same."

"Right on," he says as we both sit there, straddling our boards, bobbing over another small wave. "Don't wait too long. Only so many waves before darkness falls."

"Yeah," I chuckle at his sarcasm. It can't even be 9 a.m. yet.

As I'm about to bob over another small wave, he starts to make a move for it. "What's he doing?" I ask myself. It's a bunny hill compared to his last wave, yet he paddles on, building momentum and then pops up. "See ya Brando," he shouts, surfing away. "What… How does he know my name?" He wiggles and swerves his board with the grace of a dolphin. He seems to be riding the distance as if he's going to shore. As the wave dies he keeps paddling inland.

"Where's he going?"

Clueless about this mysterious surfer, I catch the next wave in pursuit. Although mediocre, I make the most of it, just trying to get to the beach. By the time I reach the sand he's already toweled off and throwing on a red robe.

I power walk out of the water and jog up the slanted sand to catch him. "What's up with the robes," I ask as he slips leather thongs onto his feet. "Are you some sort of surfing monk?"

"Ha, yes I am a monk. And I love surfing, so maybe I am."

"Seriously," I ask. "How do you know who I am?"

"I don't," the monk says.

"Well you know my name," I return.

"Meditation."

"What?" I question, surprised again. "You're joking right?"

"My wisdom is often times beyond me. What I know and what I do is not an attribute." He takes his thongs off and sits down in the lotus position and puts his hands on his knees.

"Dude, I have no idea what you mean," I say, looking down at him, my feet nervously shuffling in the sand.

"I am a monk as you suggested; have been for twenty years. The commitment requires me to sacrifice much of my ego, most of my own personal desires, and to practice disciplined routines. But, through meditation, it has allowed me to tap into a connection - a connection between all living things."

"Ok," I say barely understanding.

"After a recent meditation, I'm meant to give you a message, one which will help not only you, but many other people."

"This *is* a joke."

"There are only so many waves before darkness falls," the monk repeats, his dark eyes earnestly looking at me, into me as if he speaks to my soul.

"Yeah, you said that back in the water," I mention, my feet still sifting sand. "You realize it's morning right?"

"No, a greater darkness will fall," he says. "You don't need to understand it now, just hear it."

"This guy... What's he talking about?" thinking he's either mad or telepathic.

"May I show you something?" The monk holds his right hand out, palm open.

Part of me wants to lose this guy, but curiosity is as powerful a force as the ocean current. Open palmed, he points with his hand to the spot in the sand next to him, motioning for me to sit down as if he wants me to take the same cross legged posture he's easily maintaining. Oddly enough, I try and wind up in a sort of half lotus position.

"Through what I call the Connection, let me show you your death," the monk says.

"What?" Goosebumps rise on the back of my neck. "This guy's crazy," I think. "I should go."

"It is without harm," he replies. "I can take you there peacefully, through a guided meditation."

Intrigued again, "OK, why not?"

"Close your eyes and pay attention to your breathing," he says. "Your breath is your true identity. Let go of everything except your breath."

Instead of letting go of everything I cling to everything, reflecting on my surroundings: "OK the ocean is that way, in front of me; there are probably people running by; I wonder if they are looking; it's getting warmer; I should have worn sunscreen; what am I doing? I can't focus; this position is uncomfortable; this is ridiculous."

Startling – the monk shouts, "If all of humanity depended on you, would you Focus?!"

Instantly I'm greeted with such a strong idea, such a vivid vision, that I'm in a new place, a water garden. I'm standing on a lawn of damp moss at the edge of a silky smooth pond, about the size of a typical ice skating rink. Ahead, the pond ends like an infinity pool with a glass wall, the ending edge not clearly visible. Beyond the pond, I'm not sure. It's like looking over the edge of a cliff. I can't really see anything other than sky blue sky.

Floating along the top of the pond is a straight path of round stepping stones, cutting through the middle. The path is beckoning me and almost has me miss what makes the most commotion of all. Slick, mossy rock walls, about twenty feet tall, jut out of both ends of the pond to my right and to my left. Water flows down both walls creating moderately noisy waterfall sounds and ripples into and across the pond. By the time the ripples reach the floating pathway, they have nearly subsided. "Peaceful, is this heaven?" I wonder.

Even though the soothing ambiance of the trickling fountains tempts me, I don't look back because the path still beckons me. Hopping to the first floating stone, I land on one foot, balancing just enough to plant the second foot down and get stable - surfing skills. I still can't see beyond the pond, but my curiosity increases as if my destiny waits for me at the edge of the pond. Hopping to the second, I still can't see. I hop along finding each floating stone to be a bit slicker, a bit more covered in moss than the last. Getting closer, the waterfall noises grow louder. Three quarters along the way, I can start to see down below, a bit of greenery, and what looks like the tops of waterfalls facing back at me. Even on the second to the last stone, which is quite mossy, I can't see the bottom of the waterfalls. "What's down there?" I try to peer closer but to no avail.

The last stone, near the edge, is more spaced out than the rest of the stones, but I jump to it because I have to see. Landing on the last floating, mossy, stepping stone is about as difficult as you'd think it would be to land on a floating, mossy, stepping stone. I slip and fall not into the pond, but off the edge of the pond, which I've just come to know as a massive waterfall itself. "What have I done?" Panic!

In wild desperation, I flail about trying to cling to something, but I'm only met by empty air. There's absolutely nothing to grab. At an ever-increasing speed, I fall, enfolded into an expansively wide chute, surrounded by unhelpful waterfalls, all different heights and widths. The waterfall that I just slipped off, by far the widest and tallest, is nearly the entire width of that pond. Looking down, even as I fall I still can't see the bottom, just mist way down there. I might as well be sky diving. Terrified, I think, "So this is it?" As if falling to my death isn't a fast enough way to go, the bottom is so far away that I'm actually waiting to die. "I'm going to die! What about my life? Why did I…?"

As much as I regret taking that floating path, fretting is pointless because there's no hope of escaping this situation. Last moments. "What will happen? Life. Death. Anything else? Will it hurt?"

Fall.

For some reason, I notice freedom.

Mist at terminal velocity. Nothing left to do. I spread my arms like wings. Wind against my face. The feeling in my stomach. Exhilarating, ironically.

I'm enjoying this fall to my death. It's the most alive I've ever felt. My heart pounds like a drum. Now amidst the mist, I can't really see, but I don't really care. The bottom must be close.

Then I feel the solid, immovable sandy Kailua beach. The monk is to my left. The ocean is in front of me, "I'm alive." I'm relieved, but I'm relaxed.

"So that was it," I say as calmly as the monk's usual tone. "That meditation was my death."

"No, that was life. You were fearlessly living; something you must continue to do before darkness falls. And people must see you do it." The monk stands.

"Where are you going?"

"I told you what you needed to hear. Now, I must go." He slips his feet into his leather thongs and walks off.

My energy, that of a former athlete, which always felt limitless, now feels focused, as if I could harness it. I grab my board and dash into the ocean. I paddle out to the break, meeting a wave ready to cape overhead. It looks as if it wants to drown me, however, feeling synchronized with the universe, I'm ready to surf. I pop up and feel the energy, the powerful momentum of the wave. Then I feel my own energy and it feels even greater than the wave's. I swerve back and forth with the grace of a dolphin.

TRANSCENDENCE - - - - Dan AGED 63 - - - - 2010

It doesn't matter what time I go to bed. I just don't need an alarm clock. After years of rising at 3:30 a.m. to get ready for the morning news, my body clock functions on its own. These days, waking before dawn is just as normal as the fight to get back to sleep. If I do get a second nightly nap, I'm usually up by 7:30 or 8:00, washing my face, routinely staring in the mirror.

Getting up is literally like clockwork, but gourmet coffee keeps the motor running. Zombie-stepping down the hall, I softly stagger to the kitchen to brew a cup for myself and Laurie. We both like it black, no cream, and no sugar. She counts on it just as much as I do and she won't get out of bed until she smells its aroma.

After the first, hot sip of fresh fuel, I look out the kitchen window and assess the neighborhood, appreciating the morning. One of the neighbors is walking her two poodles up the cul-de-sac.

Never ready to retire, I pull out 'Dad's drawer' from the kitchen island to grab the Citizen watch Brandon, really Laurie, got me last Christmas. "I never did get a gold watch at the end of my forty year career. Anyhow, 7:56 and ready to get the day started. Come to think of it, I never received a nice, fat bonus pension either," I muse.

Carrying the coffee past Brandon's room down the hallway to the Master bedroom, I think, "it's too bad too because Brandon's caretaking bill is still steep; Chelsea's tuition is no ice cream either." Entering my bedroom, I stop my little voice from chattering away because otherwise I'll start whinging about the stock market hit we took with the current economy. Fortunately, there's been a helpful joke that's been traveling around my photography committees about how to make a small fortune in photography. It's simple. Just start with a large fortune. No matter how much I sell my photos for, there's always bills.

Mom rises from her siesta to find her cup of Joe on her bedside table and me already out the bedroom door. "Morning honey," I say walking away. "I'll be in the office."

"She'll join me in a bit," I realize. The most convenient aspect of our 'retired' lifestyle is definitely the commute. We stay close to Brandon, and work on our passion projects from home, my photography and blog; her church involvement and her writing. Her new, self published book is the reason she's joining me in the office when she gets up. Titled "Moments", it's a collection of 31 of her favorite church devotions. More than anything, it's an advent present for her mother. I'm helping out with the images, shooting 31 photographs, one for each story. "Almost done, but I still have to come up with a few more ideas," I reflect. I'm brilliantly creative,

Laurie says, but I'm running out of creativity for the time being.

Much of my photography is hung on the walls all around the house, family portraits upstairs, artistic and competition prints downstairs. I walk down our maple colored wooden stairs to the first floor. Glimpses of my work challenge me to find the next thing. Race cars, fashion-models, architecture, children, musicians, ballerinas, whatever it is, I want the image to really pop, and to tell a story. I've yet to shoot the Aurora Borealis, Polar Bears, The Bermuda Triangle, Pandas in China, Surfing Penguins in New Zealand. It's an endless list.

~ ~ ~

CHAPTER 17EVENTEEN

TRANSCENDENCE - - - - Brandon AGED 25 - - - - 2011

"The wind swirls out there." Darren Cahill, Agassi's coach, tried to give his fellow countryman, Alun, a bit of advice before he faced Nadal.

Swirls? Alun thought on his way to court. *What the hell does that mean?*

First round of the 2007 U.S. Open, at age 26, Australia's Alun Jones took on a blooming protégé, the number two seeded, Raphael, the Spanish bull, Nadal.

Nadal's career is how every other tour player wanted their careers to be shaped: A grand slam champion, an impeccable win-loss record, millions of fans, and millions of dollars. Jonesy forced himself to see Nadal in a different light. Nadal was nothing more than the next challenge.

That mindset is an innate discipline of Jonesy's, one which propelled Alun to 120 on the ATP world rankings, which in turn earned him this position in the U.S. Open. The asset allows him to 'GO' for his shots. If he makes a mistake, he laughs or shakes it off. But then he gets back to it. He stays loose, but focused.

Alun enjoyed the challenge of Nadal, but he was there to crack the top 100. He was there to win. To push the match the distance, to a deciding fifth set, he was in position to close a critical, sitter volley. However, sometimes the easy shots are the most overlooked.

Alun missed the shot. He lost to Nadal in four sets and collected $20,000 for a first round exit.

Not long after, he retired from the circuit, at a time when most of his critics say was during his prime - much too early to stop playing. But the pressures of scrapping into the top 100, the constant travel as well as the day in and day out grind, is an easy cause for burn out. That's the cut-throat nature of tennis. One must, not only be good, but master the fundamental techniques and tactics; and then be as mentally solid as a brick wall. Now at 31, he coaches at the National Tennis Center back in his home town, Canberra, Australia.

With his arms crossed, hugging his racket, he watches me and his top pupils dispersed across hard courts 2 and 3 as we warm up for another quality practice session. Behind his Nike hat and Oakley sunglasses, he watches me miss three shots in a row. He doesn't say anything, but has to look away out of disgust.

Missing three shots in a row, in front of anyone who has mastered tennis, will instill an instant lack of respect. It's not that being bad at tennis makes me a bad person, but the skill definitely reflects personality. Drill me on forehands and backhands and I'll place 99 percent near any given target on the court. So missing three consecutive shots that have been rallied directly to me is simply a lack of focus, reflecting my personality faults. It conveys a message of indecision, asking; "Who's in charge? Am I in control of my mind or is my mind in control of me? Or is my mind even present?"

Even if missing three shots in a row didn't temporarily lose Alun's respect, it certainly doesn't motivate me. "Let's go BC, bring the energy," I tell myself. "Fire up!"

Fortunately, a practice session with Alun and his Australian pupils, some of the best juniors in the world, is all about raising energy levels. Riffing is encouraged. As we get into it, we talk shit, bag one another out, or play points.

The environment is always right for it, especially with today's hit group. Jared and Jake Wynan, 19 and 17, bring their sibling rivalry anywhere they go, and are always competitive. Italian blooded, Andrew Zedde, 17, loves being in the middle of the action. And Nick Kyrgios, the biggest and loudest of us all, is the second best 16 year old in the world and wears his confidence on his sweat band.

We go straight into points as we get the session underway. "Where's a ball boy when you need one?" Nick asks, looking around for the closest ball.

"Nick, I already have one," I tell him, ready to feed in a point. "What do you want - a forehand or a backhand?"

"I don't care. They're both fucking solid," Nick retorts.

"Alright, let's see." I feed in the ball.

"Whatever old man, let's go," Nick says. I get some respect because I played in college and some respect because I'm as fit as a tri-athlete, but at 25, it's true that they look at me as if I'm aging. *Good thing I can bring the heat.*

I feed Nick a forehand and try to grind him down with consistency. We shuffle our feet around the court, loudly exhaling every time we hit a ball.

Hit, "Uhhh".

Hit, "Uhhh".

Hit, "Uhhh".

Hit,"Uhhh".

I'm consistent, but my placement isn't good enough. After just four balls, he cracks a forehand winner. We have a few more points, but I'm off. My shots sit up, giving away offense. Lucky for me, Timmy rocks up. It was a phone call to Tim, my former Australian college teammate/roommate that set up this training situation. Canberra is his hometown and Alun is a close friend.

"Timmy!" Alun hollers out as a point finishes.

"Hey Tim," another of the guys says as I walk over to him.

"Brando, mate, Wardy wants you to coach for him this afternoon," Tim says first thing. Wardy is Damien Ward, Alun's business partner and childhood friend. He played college tennis in the States for BYU and then had a brief career in the pros afterwards. He toured as a coach with top players until he and Alun took over the facility here.

"Yeah, no probs."

"OK cool, I'll let him know," he says. "So, how are you hitting?" Since college, Tim has given up competitive tennis in pursuit of a career in public motivational speaking. When I mucked around in

Vegas and Hawaii, he completed a self designed Masters' degree. He spent more than $30,000 touring to different international seminars hosted by speakers such as Tony Robbins, Wayne Dyer, T. Harve Eker, Blaire Singer, Donald Trump, Robert Kiyosaki, etc. He's starting to sound like he's one of them. But until he actually becomes such, he keeps himself busy by coaching tennis to many of Damien's and Alun's students. That and he regularly checks on my progression. I've been away from the game for two years so my progression needs to be checked.

"Uh not great actually," I answer Tim.

"Why's that?"

"I'm not sure. I feel like I was in the zone all last week, but I just can't seem to get back there. I know how to hit, and even how I could potentially hit, but I'm just not doing it."

"The zone, eh?" Tim motions for me to walk with him to the neighboring next court.

"The danger zone," I joke, following him.

There's already a basket of tennis balls on the court and Tim strolls over to it as if he wants to run me through some drills. Naturally, I walk to the other side of the court. Alun and his boys continue with points on their court.

Before Tim feeds, he asks, "What's it like when you're in the zone?"

"Everything is amazing," I say. "I can hit the ball exactly where I want, every time. I don't miss. My timing is good. I can get to every shot. I read the play well. You know, basically playing off my tits."

"OK and what does that feel like?"

"Well, it feels good of course. It feels amazing, like I'm invincible."

"Here, hit a few balls and see if you can get there," Tim says as he feeds me shots. My hitting feels clean, but not pure.

A few more and, "Nah, I'm not there, man."

Tim stops feeding. "OK, you said that last week you were in the zone. Can you remember what that was like?"

My efforts last week aren't really where I want to be. I want to be zoned in like I was when I was in all of those daydreams, like when I surfed in Hawaii, after the meditation with that monk. The fall to my death. The exhilaration in every nanosecond. To spread my arms like wings. To live. I surfed with more energy than the wave that pushed me. That's the whole reason I'm here. I've come back to tennis because it's my vehicle to really live, and to be the example. "Only so many waves before night falls." The monks words are now mine. *That's why I'm here.*

"Timmy, I need to hit better than I've ever hit. I need to hit at my full potential."

"OK, and what does –

"I know, I know - what does that feel like?" I interrupt him. "It feels like… It feels like…"

"You interrupt me and now you stutter?" Tim takes charge. "Here, hit! If you can't bloody tell me, show me!"

It's like slow motion. The first ball comes over the net, it's yellow fuzz exposed, the HEAD Practice logo enlarged. My racket swings forward like a wrecking ball. Bounce, hit. The collision is an explosion…

*

Is that Nadal on the other side of the net? The stadium is packed with people. A padded feeling underfoot…grass…*I'm at Wimbledon!* My racket swings forward like a wrecking ball. I jet a forehand down the line, exhaling, "uh,eehhhh!" It's a winner! Half of the crowd stands, and cheers "Novak". *They cheer for me?*

In the heat of the moment, instincts pump my arms like the air-lawnmower. "Come on!" The crowd cheers harder. Energy…

*

I'm still center court at Wimbledon…Is that Novak on the other side of the net? …the feeling of long hair held back by a bandana, swathing against the back of my neck…lunge into a slide to retrieve, converting risky defense into impossible offense… … heavy topspin comes off of my racket… "EEAAAhhhhhh!" *I'm Nadal?*

The crowd is into it. Energy is through the roof…

*

…Rory McElroy, torque, unleashed, pendulum swing…contact on a glossy, white, little meteorite. "Wwuuhhhh!" The energy of the flight…

*

…Dirk Nawinsky - gigantic energy, gracefully harnessed. "Weufff!" The ball - swoosh.

*

…Cadel Evans - sleeking over pavement, sppppuuurrrr. "Phuh, phuh, phuh, phuh, phuh, phuh, phuh."

*

"Match point," Tim yells out to signal that it's the last ball in the basket.

Crack!

Tim puts his racket in the basket and claps his hands together. "That was it! That's a moment of brilliance if I've ever seen one."

The boys on the other court have stopped, jaws dropped, their reactions giving me goose bumps.

"That was big hitting!" Alun exclaims.

"Brando, you're a spastic," Jake banters. "Where did that come from?"

TRANSCENDENCE - - - - Chelsea AGED 24 - - - - 2011

"He's not living!" I yell at my Smartphone, gaining a small audience at the Long Beach Performing Arts Center. "Cool it, Chels," I tell myself as I step outside, trying to avoid sharing my frustrations with perfect strangers.

The Long Beach Performing Arts Center is hosting TED (Technology, Entertainment and Design), the nonprofit organization with the mission to spread brilliant ideas. They organize many of the world's most fascinating thinkers-n-shakers to share their ideas in presentations of 20 minutes or less.

Renowned teacher, Sir Ken Robinson, spoke here on the subject of schools suppressing creativity. Al Gore has been here speaking about the global climate crisis. Famous musicians show up to show off; so do scientists, photographers, humanitarians and a few of your average Nobel Prize or Fields Medal candidates. Fun social tools, futuristic technology, there is always more that's new and different: Joyride, the self-driving Google car; explore the space hotel blueprints from Richard Branson; et cetera.

Gates is back again this year. "Maybe I'll make it to BG's talk, maybe not," I contemplate. Many of the speakers are here for a global cause-to help the globe survive worsening economic and agricultural conditions. Global resources decrease and population increases. By 2050 earth's human population is predicted to be over 9 billion. But I don't give a crap about money, and my brain doesn't register the number "9 billion" when I look at Brandon. I'm here for the neuroscientists.

Resonating through my iPhone, Mom's voice reassures, "He is living."

"You can hardly say he has a life."

"Honey, he's living the life God planned for him," Mom replies, obviously satisfied with such justification.

"*This* is not good enough," I dispute. "He's more than a freaking quarter century old. Your kids are now adults. For how long is this going to continue?"

The I-405 traffic grows noisier as I walk further from the building.

"It's natural to combat God's plan when we don't understand, but we have got to live in faith. We won't always have full perspective." It's hard to argue with her when her lawyer is God.

"Mom, he's almost 26."

"Chelsea, life is short. Enjoy what you can and be truly glad because joy is ahead." I feel like I'm talking to the Bible. "I can't do this.

"Let's talk about something else." I try to exhale my stress away. "Anyway, what are you doing today?" I check my Invicta. *I'll chat just a little longer and then head back in.*

"Your father and I are practicing our Mandarin."

"Mandarin? Why Mandarin?" I ask, persistently astonished by Mom and Dad. "That's not exactly a common hobby."

"Your father and I are going to China."

"Cool! Random! When did y'all decide this?"

"Oh, well, we just decided... We're going in September." Mom sneezes.

"Bless you. And can I come?"

"Thank you and no, sorry, we already have our tickets. Brandon's not even joining us. He's staying back with Cassandra."

"OK, well fine. That should be a fun trip."

"I know, right? Nihao, wo xiang bingshui," Mom jokingly pronounces.

"Try that in Spanish," I challenge Mom.

"Hello, I want ice water!" she over-annunciates laughing, happy with herself.

"¡Que bueno!" I chuckle with her, "At least you'll be well hydrated."

"You're right. Maybe I should learn how to get to a bathroom!" Mom cracks me up, "What are you up to, chickadee?"

"On a break right now. There's another speaker I want to catch in about five minutes."

"You're at TED?" Mom acts surprised.

"Yeah, remember?"

"Oh, I didn't realize it was this week. I was picturing you still at school."

"You should know. You paid for it."

"Oh right—the credit card bill hasn't hit, yet," she says cheerily. "I can't believe that's all you wanted for your birthday."

"Well, I appreciate it. Actually, I should get going. That talk really is starting soon."

"OK, well I hope you're enjoying yourself. Are you? What's it like?"

Not wanting to hang up, I walk and talk. "It's informative; it really is. I just came out of a presentation from a popular neuroscientist, Damasio. He spoke about brain functions during decision-making. It was interesting, but I'm not sure it will help my research for Brandon."

"Oh honey! You're so good. You're doing too much."

"No! ¡No te preocupes! I'm getting credit towards my Masters' here. The whole weekend counts."

She sighs the way only moms can, "I think you overburden yourself." "She's relentless—concerned. Be sincere, Chels," I chide myself.

"I'm fine, but thank you. I'm going to sign off, but I'll call you later. Love you." Walking into the next conference room, I wonder if I am doing too much. *But he's my brother! I am my brother's keeper.*

"Thank you," I say to the older gentleman holding the door for me.

TRANSCENDENCE - - - - Laurie AGED 54 - - - - 2011

I ordered it. I knew I was getting it. Maybe it's the similarity in how the spoon and bowl are displayed. The pea soup in front of me evokes a flashback. Brandon as a toddler sits in his highchair in the kitchen as I put a bowl of pea soup in front of him. I briefly turn away to check the roasting turkey, and reset the timer on the oven. I turn back to find Baby Brando in action as he flings a spoonful of pea soup against the wall. His mucky ammunition splatters. *He's flung soup all over the wall!*

Peppering my soup as the bowl ever so slightly slides a centimeter on the train's tray top table, I reminisce. When *Brandon was a child, he always had a way to advertise his annoyances.* He didn't want that green mush. He wasn't one to throw a tantrum, but he'd pout if he didn't like something, or he'd throw it.

When I brought him into this world he didn't talk. I'd talk, and he'd make baby sounds. We still had our mother-son communication. Whether a sigh, a cry, or a laugh, his non-verbal cues were just as strong as words.

Every day after his day care I'd pick him up and put him in his car seat. I'd talk to him. I'd ask him what he wanted for dinner.

"Hotdog" His first word!

"Hotdogs it is" I answered.

I knew his first word was coming, but it seemed early. I didn't know when it would actually happen.

Then, as he grew into a young child, he was very acute. He was a chatter box. Now, when he talks, he has me on the edge of my seat. It's like he's saying his first word all over again.

Sleek as a silver bullet, Harmony, the 'bullet train' usually makes the 1,300 kilometer spree from Beijing to Shanghai in less than five hours. Our trip is literally on the tracks to make the same time. Our carriage is similar to the inside of an airplane. Our seats recline, we have in-seat entertainment systems, and attendants march up and down the aisle to handle food service.

The pea soup is good, but it's unsettling. I miss the kids.

An hour and a half into the trip and the immediate scene outside the window is still opaque. A panorama of the dark Taihang Mountain range is in the distance. Our train cruises alongside blurred landscape which creates a perfect setting for 'brain-wandering'. In my head, I relive the past week where we lollygagged in Beijing. It was an ideal introduction to China.

Despite the fact that the city of 19 million people has become modernized over recent years, taxi-cabs have replaced more and more bicycles, and high-rises stand where once ancestral architecture existed, tradition still stands. The city is now a mash-up and that's how we decided to see it. We stayed in a small hotel with a Szechuan theme, where a common courtyard is shared by the surrounding buildings. That and rented bicycles to get around made the busy city seem homier. Aside from testing out old fashioned local living, we also did the typical tourist site seeing which included visiting Tiananmen Square, the Forbidden City and the Great Wall of China. We were bowled over by the fact that the sites that created such a tremendous impact at their first inception remain just as much an impact to those of us lucky enough to see them today.

"What are we doing here honey?" I ask Dan, after downing another spoonful of pea soup.

He looks up from his digital camera roll. "We're going to Shanghai."

"Yes, I know, but I mean here in China. Why didn't we bring the kids?"

"Oh. Well we have to let them grow up dear."

"What about us? Are we just old, traveling retirees? Traveling was meant to bring us together as a family."

"Well it's bringing us together."

"Oh I know," I kick him.

"And I wouldn't say we are old for retirees. We are about average." Dan puts down the camera, puts his arm around me, and gives me a smirk. "What's bringing this about?"

After pausing to carefully phrase my words, "I'm not complaining because I love the life we have. I love you, and our family, and the future we continue to grow into, but I feel like we've fallen into a comfort zone."

"I'm not," Dan jokes. "I'm *reclining* into a comfort zone."

"Ha, ha," I say obnoxiously. "I really want us to dedicate ourselves to something."

"What about church?" Dan looks out the window. "You're more involved than most."

"Yes, but I think we can do more, so much more."

He looks at me and cheekily questions, "*We*?"

"Well it was fun working on the last two photography books together, don't you think?" He nods, ready to hear where I'm going.

"So I had an idea. You know that lady from your BNI group?" BNI, Business Networking International, is a franchised organization of which Dan's been a member for the past four years.

"Which lady?"

"That lovely lady who owns the travel agency."

"You mean Peri," Dan confirms. "Yeah, she planned the day with the pandas we are getting next week."

"Yes, Peri," I answer. "We chatted during that dinner party last year about the Africa trip we took. She said she liked the idea behind mission trips and said she would help us out if we ever wanted to do another one."

"Well that was through St. Matt's," Dan rebuts. "How could Peri help?"

"I want to start a nonprofit organization, separate from church -"

"Oh great," Dan sarcastically interrupts.

"...and the purpose of the organization is to promote travel, and also connections between people. I want to live in a world where people consider themselves in a global community."

Dan quietly considers my thought. I know what he's going to say.

"And what is our role?"

"Our role is as a husband and wife journalist team. We will publicize stories of the organization's missions," I answer. "For it to work though, we need to enroll other people."

~ ~ ~

CHAPTER 18IGHTEEN

TRANSCENDENCE - - - - Brandon AGED 27 - - - - 2012

A prosperous performance on the men's circuit is rewarded with ranking points. An accumulation of those points allows players to move up through the three tiers of tournaments, Futures, Challengers and finally the ATP tour events.

Usually fans at the Futures are scarce, but small crowds and their transfixed eyes solicit my matches. Since Australia, here in Valldoreix, and every tournament in between, this has been the case. They're attracted to my intensity.

In between a game, up 6-2, 5-2, I wonder what they must see; some grimy, mud dog, something that emerged from the back of this clay court, existing only to play the match. My opponent mopes about as if it's not fair to get matched up against an animal. I think he's somewhat expecting me to lap up a slurp of mud-puddle water instead of sipping PowerAde.

Time to zone in again.

Serving out the last game, I see open targets. It's pressure on the gas, pedal to the floor, sixth gear. I'm in a Lamborghini with unlimited jet fuel. I couldn't expel my energy even if I wanted to.

I hit a big, well placed serve up the T. My eyes calibrate on the ball and a contact point for it and my racket. I am the full extension of my racket's reach. Serve. Return. Forehand crosscourt. Rallied back. Forehand down the line. Rallied back. Forehand angle. Scraped back. Closing swinging volley. Dictation just happened.

Three points from the win, in starting my service motion, the lights go out...

In complete blackness, paused from the journal entry, I drop my pen...

VISION - - - - Dan AGED 66 - - - - 2012

Dave and Sandy have taken time away from Name Brand Marketing to lead tonight's event, though they debated whether to begin the evening by plunging straight into business or allowing time for the guests to bond first. I think they made the right choice by first holding this casual 'meet and greet' dinner where the overall project will be unveiled.

The Spanish Colonial dining room is proving to be a comfortable venue for this gathering; Dave deftly works one side of the room, Sandy the other.

Both of them hand out booklets that tell the story of our non-profit, HowYaTraveling. They make eye contact with each potential investor. *These guys are always ready for business.*

Watching the action is like watching a business ballet: poised, calculated, and focused. Laurie and I quietly watch the performance from one side of the room, especially keeping an eye on a table near the front of the room. That's where Peri - the travel agent from BNI, who orchestrated this Bermuda retreat, holds court. Peri is a detail person who effectively caters to the needs of the VIPs in attendance. At her table at this moment is Belinda King from King Corporate, James Peters from UK Investments and Steven Michelson from New York. Each is a power-hitter. Each could single handedly underwrite our entire project. But that isn't the point here tonight. *Raising money to help those in need is not only a personal satisfaction but also a responsibility that all caring people share. In this case, Laurie and I want to gather support from as many people as possible, instead of a lone fat-cat investor. Hopefully this little clam bake does the trick.*

Two waiters, formally dressed in white, tactfully move around Dave and Sandy and their gathering. They're to enhance the intimacy of the moment as they serve bread and refill water glasses. "No ice; am I correct Sir?" Alvin makes sure as he fills a water glass. All of the employees at the Coco Reef Resort are trained as actors. Hotel owner, John Jeffries, makes sure of that. He is renowned for claims that he has built gorgeous sets and backdrops, and his staff shall warmly interact with the hotel's guests. "Hopefully many of you will become stars in their eyes," Jeffries comments every time he meets new employees.

Speaking of whom, Mr. Jeffries walks into the room alongside the hotel manager. I think Peri previously mentioned that Mr. Jeffries likes to be involved with most of the functions hosted by his properties. No wonder he's the multiple winner of the annual World Travel Award for interior design and superior service.

In a black dress shirt with subtle glossy black trim around the edge of the collar, standing about 6'1, Jeffries patiently waits next to the hotel manager a few paces inside of the double door entrance as if to build anticipation. He has a receding hairline, yet well kempt grey hair. His face is tan and bears a ceaseless smile. He has already captivated the room's attention. "Hello, I'm John Jeffries and this is our lovely hotel manager, Carmel Guerra."

"Hello," Carmel waves. She snuggly presses against the inside seams of her own blazer jacket and skirt. A rosy, larger woman with high cheek bones and blonde hair, she looks like a retired model who ate too many cream puffs.

"I am the owner of this hotel and I am always honored when I have the chance to meet my guests. Carmel informed me that this is the first visit for all of you. I hope you find your stay memorable."

"Here, here." Some of the group praises. "Cheers."

"Cheers."

Jeffries, who has a splash of Hollywood showmanship about him, continues, "Carmel has also told me that for those of you who are feeling adventurous, there will be scuba diving in the morning. It should be very exciting."

"That is right." Carmel cheerfully smiles.

"I would also like to invite you to my fine art gallery tomorrow evening," he adds. "We are putting on a show featuring a variety of Caribbean artists. Some of the artwork, I must say, is exquisite. I look forward to seeing and meeting many of you there. Other than that, have a wonderful time in Bermuda. If you need anything at all, just let us know. If I am not around, our lovely hotel manager here should be." Mr. Jeffries nods his head.

Carmel beams. "Consider me your bosom buddy," she says in a Swedish accent, giggling like Mrs.

Clause. She waves, again, and exits with Mr. Jeffries back through the double doors. As they walk away, much of our group acknowledges their courtesies.

Dave and Sandy, meantime, have left a stack of promotional folders with each potential investor and returned to their table just to the left of ours.

Laurie stands.

"What nice people," she says referring to Mr. Jeffries and Carmel. "I'm not usually one for speeches, but I want to propose a toast. I want to thank everyone for coming. We're here tonight, in the middle of the Atlantic, because we share a common love, not only for traveling, but a love for connecting with other people and other places. Everyone here understands that value from first-hand experiences."

Most in the room nod.

"The mission of HowYaTraveling is to promote a global-community perspective. Dan and I only hope to initiate such a goal with deep seeded connections that begin this weekend. Again, thanks again for being here. Prost. Here's to connections." Laurie raises her glass.

"Cheers."

"Prost."

The waiters glide into the softly lit hall to get ready to serve dinner; gourmet delicacies from the hotel's signature restaurant, Juanito's. The theme is a tribute to Juan de Bermudez, the Spanish explorer who discovered Bermuda in 1505 and gave his name to the islands. The menu seems limitless with an extensive array of foods to satisfy the diversity of pallets in this worldly crowd. Laden with pear fruit salads, braised chicken, escargot and swordfish, each meal is artistically presented and designed to please.

As I dig into my dinner and engage in small talk with Laurie and Peri, who has joined us, and the rest of our table, I contemplate the challenge that lies ahead as we craft a unified global mission and at the same time meet specific goals required by many of the potential investors.

Belinda King, a redheaded woman, who now sits at a table in the corner accompanied by her two personal aids, is the owner of an investment company very willing to invest, but she wants hands-on involvement. James Peters from UK Investments, over there, is just as interested to invest, but is also interested in a return. Many of the potential investors want the organization to go public. They want to be stakeholders. Some of the investors are wealthy philanthropists looking for tax write-offs, but also looking for a trustworthy organization. We have a variety of situations to look at, but one thing true of all of the potential investors is that they are willing to participate in the mission trips. "That's sincere faith in investment," I believe.

This tropical setting at the Coco Reef Resort proves to be a soothing environment for both business and pleasure. Far away from the usual din, we've set up camp on a meticulously manicured estate outside Hamilton City. At hotel's edge, the beach is a luxurious blend of white sand and carpet-thick lawns, leading into the crystal clear Caribbean Sea. And even though this hotel seems intimate, there are more than seventy suites here along with an atrium lobby, a multi-level terrace that leads to a pool and the Vista Bar with a balcony.

After dinner, Laurie and I find ourselves mingling with Hugo Wight, an African pastor who now preaches at a national church in Savannah, Georgia. His church has been seeking unique ways to add charitable contributions to the world. We had already heard that Hugo had similar ideas about how travel can create important links among peoples and nations. Our conversation carries us into an ornate atrium lobby just outside the dining room. The lobby features remarkable statues and fountains, some ancient, some stylized to blend in with the current decor. The 6,000 square foot tile floor makes an intricate mosaic. I remember reading in the brochure that the marble was brought in from a unique Jamaican quarry.

"I came here directly from Jamaica," Hugo says, disregarding the floor in order to observe the atrium's fifty foot ceiling. "I met with other ministers. Some of them were from other faiths as well. My effort was to find a common ground in spirituality."

"Ah, the acceptance as a Christian," Laurie exclaims.

"Well yes ideally," Hugo says. "I even met with many spiritual people of the Rasta culture, many of whom happen to be role models in Jamaica."

"How about Bob Marley?" Laurie asks.

"Yes, Bob Marley too. Over there, he was not just a Reggae product, but extremely influential. He was very much a man of God."

"Sure, I've heard that," I say in sincerity. "I've heard he's considered a prophet to some."

"A prophet?" Laurie says sarcastically.

"Yeah, really," Hugo reassures. "Vision, I learned, is what Rastafarianism is all about. It's the vision that life is a gift and keeping that vision all of the time is essential. It instructs us to live in righteousness, and in natural love of mankind. And that is a message I can help spread."

"We'd be happy to jump on board with a message like that too," I comment, walking the three of us back into the dining room.

We approach a group of three young men in fitted suits. I assume they are from the Society of Young Philanthropists.

"Ah, the Christophers," one of the young men says. Strong jaw line, he's mid twenties; about 6'4 and wearing a single breasted grey suit with dual buttons and pointed lapels. "I'm Ryan Greer."

"Nice to meet you," we greet him and the other two young men. "Where are you from?"

"We are from Dallas," Ryan says,

"Ooh that's a busy city," Laurie jokes.

"Yes, but we get away enough," Ryan says. "In fact Thomas here, was just saying how he started traveling with his family when he was as young as four." When I look at Thomas, the first thing I notice is his Grease Lightning black Italian hair.

"And I still love to travel," Thomas says, his enthusiasm shining through his smile. "We all do. It's a major reason for us wanting to help your organization."

"That's wonderful. Thank you," Laurie says. "Traveling is often an awakening experience."

"It is, yes," Thomas says. "We have many friends who don't travel and the only perspectives they have of the rest of the world is from TV or the net, but it's just not the same."

"No it's not the same as connecting with someone in real life, is it?" Laurie looks at me and smiles as if she's proud of us being here.

"So, have you solved any other world problems tonight?" I say, goading Ryan, Thomas, and the other young man, Peter.

"Well, actually we were dispelling rumors about the Bermuda Triangle," Peter says with a child-like giggle. "Ryan said he'd be down to take a boat out into the Triangle and as soon as his compass goes haywire, drop anchor, and then dive to the bottom where he'll find the lost city of Atlantis."

"Ah the magnetic anomaly tactic," Laurie jokes.

"No, I only kid," Ryan says.

"You never know," I laugh. "We can get scuba certified tomorrow."

We split off finding other people to chat with. Part of me wonders what it would be like if Brandon could have this type of societal involvement. He's near the same age of those three young men.

Then suddenly, before I can get onto my next thought, the dining room is plunged into pitch black. Not a flicker of light anywhere. A mutual gasp.

"Well, that changes the mood," someone jokes.

There is a wave of nervous mutters. Concerns. A few whispers. I look for the window, but there is nowhere to look. I can't see anything, not inside, not outside. I hold up my hand in front of my face, but, I see nothing. *Oh No. Have I just lost my sight?* Panic.

My mind woolgathers for an explanation. An awkward murmur continues. There's a sense of gloom. Little movement, as we wait for the lights to return.

The seemingly endless darkness continues. It's only been a minute, but if another minute passes like this, we'll go into hysterics. I know I might. *What in the hell is happening?*

TRANSCENDENCE - - - - Brandon AGED 27 - - - - 2012

As if a stronger force moons me away from writing another letter, my pen drops from my hand mid word. Darkness inhibits my journal entry.

It's pitch black everywhere, my bedroom, where the window is, out the window. *But it's daytime.* Sitting in my desk chair aware of the eerie moment and engrossed in darkness, I wait. *Why can't I see?* I dance with concerns. *Where are Mom and Dad? Bermuda, right. Where's Cassandra? Is this real?*

Then a rush of energy knocks me out of my chair to the floor. A flash.

*

London's evening suddenly turned black. The stage lights are out. Everything's completely black. *Did I lose my sight?* Chris Martin's voice, even with the help of the microphone, is barely audible over a frightened stadium crowd. *It's not just me then. Is this a power outage? Is this a prank on the Olympics?*

"Hey, my lighter doesn't work," a voice next to me says over the growing mania.

"My mobile is out," another voice says.

"Oh my God, I can't see," another voice says.

"My torch doesn't work."

"What's happened?"

The realization that no one can create any sort of sight quickly dawns on more than 80,000 people.

Mass delirium.

Screams amplify.

"Armageddon," people shout. "2012."

Thud! "Oh that freaking hurt," I say, grabbing the back of my head. "Who hit me?"

"Oh," I cry out, again, as something like an elbow jabs my ribs. The crowd is frantic. *This is chaos.*

*

It should be daybreak, but there's no sun. There are no stars either. Nothing is visible, not even the trees. Where's the tribe? My sight! My sight! I try to look back at the hut, but I only see dark. It's like my eyes are shut, but they're not.

*

This damn maze was disorienting enough, but now an eclipse? Wait, is this one of Uncle Charlie's tricks? Wait, no. I can't see a thing. Have I gone blind?

"Sara, what's going on?"

"I don't know, but I can't see anything at the moment," she replies. "Can you? I hate the dark. Why's it so dark?"

*

Heroically claiming my freedom, checking the last of the bucket list, overcoming my lifelong fear of heights, I yell out, "BBUUUNNNNGGGEEEEE-*What on earth? I can't see. Is this a dream?*

There's no mistaking this plunging feeling. I can't see!

*

My first time skydiving, here it goes. Whoa! I can't see. The wind roars like a highway. My hands feel their way to Erica. "Mark," she yells out. "I can't see."

"I'm here," I yell back. "Wait you can't see, either?"

"You can't see?"

"No, no light, nothing."

"When do we pull the chord?"

*

"What the –

I fiddle around for the radio. Even the plane lights are out.

"Ground Control, this is Cessna 174, Pilot Andrews. Emergency. I've lost visibility."

"Roger that, lights are out. I don't –

"This is Glider Pilot Julian Gilbert. I'm in a black hole up here," another call fills the operator's background.

"My plane is out. The sky is out," I hear yet another background voice says.

"Holy shit!"

*

"Msholozi, Mscholozi, what should we do?"

"Frankly, I am not sure."

"What about South Africa?"

"I don't know what this is."

*

The light went out, but a heat blast from the blazing fire still burns against my face. It's horrifying not being able to see it. I can't see anything. The sound of the walls cracking on the second story indicates that the fire still eats away at the house.

"What should we do?" I yell over to Jason.

No response.

The sound of the blasting hose snakes about as if he's dropped it.

"What?" Hank yells. "What the hell is going on?"

*

Earth, which usually glows a bright cerulean, is gone. It's black. Our space station is black, too. Either that or we've all gone blind.

"Commander Scott, call Houston."

TRANSCENDENCE - - - - Laurie AGED 56 - - - - 2012

The oddity in the sudden loss of sight, my awareness has strangely heightened. If I could just calm myself. *Think it through, Laurie.* Although everything drowns in darkness, I still know where the tables and chairs are. I can still picture the arched windows and the ocean view beyond them. I can picture the tile border that spans along the tops of the walls. I can reasonably guess where everyone stands and sits.

"Dan," I say reaching about for his hand. I'm sure both of us share the same sense of claustrophobia, the darkness inescapable. I find his hand as he says, "I'm here". At least it's comforting to know we are all still here.

"Ok, what is this?" a man's voice pipes up, annoyed. *Maybe an investor I haven't met yet,* I think, trying to place his identity. "Are we going to do something about this?"

"What do you suggest?" Another unrecognizable voice answers. "It seems we've been thrown into the magician's black hat."

The room stays relatively quiet, everyone pondering the question.

"Well we have to do something," someone says.

"Uh I can't take this," a woman cries.

It's an eerie moment and nothing brings comfort. It's a genesis type of moment, it's so dark. *God needs to bring the light back. Is this the rapture?* I think about it for a second and realize the moment feels disturbingly evil. "Darkness was upon the face of the deep," I whisper to myself quoting the Bible's first chapter. The circumstances have forced me to stretch my mind in ways I've never before had to. *I miss the sun. I hope Earth doesn't start to freeze over. Did we get sucked into a black hole?* The thoughts upset me worse than a sour odor.

A fatigue permeates me, and I sense, everyone in the room. Dan's grip slightly weakens. *Or is it mine?* My juice is drained like a low battery.

"I'm buggered," faintly comes from someone else in the room.

"Whoa, did you guys just take an energy hit?" I ask, thirsting for rest.

"I'm done in."

"Yeah," someone else sighs.

"Same here," another whispers.

"Oh my heart," An older sounding man wheezes. "I need to lie down." I wonder if we are dying as I hear him collapse. Someone else gasps. *Is this darkness the shadow of death?*

My concern widens. I talk. I have nothing to say, but I feel like I'm cornered against a wall. "People, wait, wait. Just everybody wait. Just hold on," I say, exhausted. I know I'm talking, but I'm not sure what I'm saying. Then, a vision overrides. It's not light either, but it's like what happened in Jerusalem.

*

Smothered in darkness in the midst of dark outer space and a dark globe, Unicorn, a $2.2 billion CIA reconnaissance satellite, maintains a complex elliptical orbit at half pace. The satellite is designed to photograph large surface areas of Earth, sometimes the size of entire continents, and then determine the locations of sources of certain microwave transmissions. It also utilizes electro-optical digital imaging for real-time observation. Unicorn's zoom capability can capture areas as small as one inch.

With a dark universe, the only thing transmitting anything at all is coming from coordinates 32.275606 Latitude and -64.773447 Longitude. It's a spot on the Earth with a lit message, the only light in the universe. It's also the most concentrated energy in one place so Unicorn captures it because it recognizes it as physical activity.

The lit message emits enough energy that a portion transfers to Unicorn which zooms in for a close-up and also wirelessly transmits the feed to Langley. Along with the signal, Unicorn also transfers energy that was included with the message. Monitors inside the CIA headquarters suddenly light, but very dimly and, display a live feed of the message.

The director of national security happens to be on site with many other employees who stand in the International Communications room. They stand there fatigued, trying to understand and solve the darkness disaster, as they receive a sudden space to earth transmission of the image. Their first thoughts focus on the possibility of a hacker.

"Someone must be holding the world at ransom!" But trying to logically pin any hacker with the ability to control the sun is a bit farfetched. Unexpectedly, the message brings some relief by way of empowerment. They decide it should not be kept locked away along with their usual secrets.

"This message is giving us hope. Let's get it to the masses." The director voices an excitement that had been vanishing.

The CIA does their part.

"This image will be better known than $E=mc^2$."

They create a still image and send the message to news sources worldwide. They use a spider program to attach the image to a document being sent to every email address ever created. They wire into telecommunications satellites and send mass picture messages to the global public's mobile phones. They use other orbiting satellites to put the message in people's GPS systems. Then, the message goes viral enough to hit word of mouth. Within fifteen minutes it's the most talked about topic on the planet.

Along with the image, the energy spreads. Energy grows among the people in the International Communications room. It grows in the rest of the building, and around the world, as the image is sent, received, seen, and talked about more and more. A collective thought radiates uniformly in all directions, waves, watts, joules, energy. Worldwide, people collectively consider the same thing, and it gains them energy.

Slowly, dim amber light begins to buzz. It sounds like a faint transformer box. Then, the darkness slightly brightens. It begins to clear…

*

"Honey, honey, what are you saying?" I hear Dan's voice. I realize I'm back in the darkness of the resort. I'm not sure what I was saying, but I know what to do now.

"I know what to do," I say. "Follow me. Everyone, we are going to the beach," I start to feel around to safely make my way outside. "Honey, come on."

"Wait…where? Why the beach?" Someone grumbles.

"Just trust me," I say with calm sternness.

I hear whines, but at least they follow as I feel my way outside.

We make for a confused and tired mob stumbling through the dark as we approach the wooden walkway that leads down to the beach. Much of the walk way is composed of little plateau steps in random places and in varied amounts. When we first arrived I thought of this as a charming center piece in the middle of a well watered, elegant lawn with luxurious plants and chiseled statues. In the dark though, the walkway is an accident waiting to happen. With single beam, flimsy railings, and a potential fall down a step or maybe two.

"Take your shoes off for better footing," I softly order.

It's a wobbly trek, and though blind, we make our way down, all the while we entertain a curious hope. As soon as I step onto the sand I hurriedly scuttle around, hunting for the barbeque grill. I can't find it.

"I need help guys. Find the barbeque pit," I appeal to the others. I hear only murmurs in response.

I thought it was this way, but I feel disoriented. I try to listen for the ocean, but I can't tell where it comes from. *I'm still so tired. I miss the kids. I hope Brandon is ok. When did I let go of Dan's hand?*

"Dan," I softly call out. *Why did I bring us to the beach, I wonder? I don't –*

"I found it," I recognize the voice of Mr. Jeffries. I didn't know he was with us, but what a savior.

"Where are you?" I yell out.

"I'm over here. Follow my voice. It's me, Mr. Jeffries." Walking over to him is the scariest game of Marco Polo.

"Everyone get to Mr. Jeffries."

"Oh!"

"Owe." I collide into someone. "Sorry."

"Sorry," a lady says at the same time.

"Laurie," she says.

"Yeah," I say.

"It's Peri."

"Peri, oh Peri. Let's find Mr. Jeffries."

Through the dark abyss we make it to the barbeque pit. "Mr. Jeffries, we need the coal, the bag of coal, and lighter fluid and matches," I say.

"Everybody over here," Peri calls.

"Uh, uh, oh found 'em. Over here," Mr. Jeffries says.

"Good, come on over here to the open beach," I respond.

I hear most of the group catch up. "Ok, let me see the bag," I tell Mr. Jeffries. I hear the thick paper bag crinkling around the coals as it follows my voice. I throw my hands in that direction and come up with the heavy bag and accessories.

"Got it?" he asks.

"Yeah," I say. "Everyone give me some space."

"What's happening?" Someone asks.

"There's a message I need to spell out," I mutter in response. Our crowd is still confused and tired and I'm not giving much explanation. They barely hold for me as I do my best to blindly spread the bag of coals.

"What are we doing out here?" Someone impatiently asks.

"I'm writing human sized brail out here," I retort. The guesswork of spelling in the dark when possibly the whole world is relying on my efforts is frustrating to say the very least.

Several stressful moments later, "Ok that should do it," I say. "Everybody come to me. Follow my voice." I go through a process of finding people and guide them to the standing-room-only space surrounding my message. Again, it's mostly guess work.

"Laurie," Dan says.

"Dan, oh, there you are," I say with relief. "Stay with me."

Once we are gathered around the message I spray all of the lighter fluid and then clench the match box, feeling my thumb around for the rough lighting strip. *I don't know if this will work.* I strike a match. "Pheeoo," it burns but only weakly barely emitting heat, and no light.

"Even the fire from your match doesn't light," Someone faintly complains. "I can hear it, but no light." It's true.

I drop the match to an area that I'm pretty sure is covered with charcoal that's doused with lighter fluid. The charcoal feebly hisses and rumbles. I start to feel a little heat from it. At least we know there's fire there.

"Still no light, this isn't going to work," someone else complains. "I feel some heat, but no light."

I try to think of what to say next. This idea has to work. It's got to reach its potential. Not really knowing where I'm going with this, I start talking. "Listen, just listen to me. Listen to me for one second. I'm only a little lady in my fifties. I, I…" I stutter not sure of the words to say. I can't tell them I just had a vision. I wish I could see their faces. In a moment of truth, I question my own authority. *Do I have us pointlessly standing around scattered coals on the beach? Is this real?*

Then worse, I start thinking I could be having some sort of psychotic episode. *Was that vision real? I'm not delirious am I? I don't want to be in this place any more. How do we get out of here? Am I suddenly in hell as we've turned into wandering, faceless ghosts?*

But, then spirit sparks. A vision flashes, a millisecond of light, and then I know what to do again. I feel a surge of energy, inspiration just enough to carry me through this task.

I go on again, "The only reason you followed me out here is because this darkness is so frightening that it's become a terror. It's misery. We all ache for relief. Energy leaves us and we are *weary*. And what's on all of our minds, but none of us wants to say, is that we are dying.

"You followed me out here because you had a hope that there might actually be relief to this situation. That hope is something that I need everyone to cling to, especially, as you listen to what I'm asking you to do. Please listen to me now, because I'm absolutely serious. There is a message we have to get out to the world – the same message that I blindly wrote with this barbeque charcoal. The way we are going to do that is by lighting this fire. And we're going to light this fire with our minds."

"This has to be a joke," a voice raspier than the Godfather whips. At this point, I'm wondering if half of the group is asleep because I make out the sound of what sounds like snoring zombies.

Trying to explain, I continue. "I had just enough hope to write this message and I have just enough hope to tell you about it. Ok, bear with me. Let me tell you about something more personal - my faith in God.

"Once I was just a young mother who had to be talked into going to church. Now, I believe in Jesus and God and heaven and hell as much as I believe in Earth. Christianity is not a concept to me, but a truth. And I've often felt that it's my life purpose to spread that truth. I'll admit that any day.

"Sometimes though, my faith in God is so strong that I forget about myself. I forget to use that strength in myself. And if I didn't know any better, I would never use that strength at all.

"But when I think about it, I know it's there. Every time I look, there's strength to be found, waiting for me to tap into it. And it's always plentiful enough to take on whatever task I'm facing. That strength is the same as the hope that pushed us here, now.

"The same hope that pushed you to follow me down here, I need you to use right now. We are in a bleak situation. We need to look deep inside ourselves and we have to look for a source of energy. If we don't, we die. If we do, then we will find enough energy to surface. And we will find enough to give to this fire.

"Now I will summon my own strength, my own energy, but we all need to try. This has got to be collective. What do you guys say?!"

"OK!" Two people say at the same time as if there is nothing better to do.

"OK! Let's do it." Hugo shouts.

"Yes, good, let's make it happen!" I enthusiastically say.

Then, more of the group recognizes my energy as if it was a recently found dog that had been lost, and we get noisier.

"OK! OK! Let's do it." Excitement rises.

"Yeah, come on we have to!"

"Yeah, this is real!" someone enthusiastically shouts. "This is for the world. Let's light this fire. Light, light, light…"

We all optimistically chant, forty plus voices in unison, "light, light, light, light, light, light…" My own energy has sky rocketed. I'm the motivator and I'm the motivated. I feel alive. I feel joy. I feel power.

"Light, light, light, light…"

And then, miraculously, an obscure looking message, illuminating in charcoaled amber, is the most spirited thing I've ever seen. BE THE LIGHT.

~ ~ ~

CHAPTER 19INETEEN

TRANSCENDENCE - - - - Chelsea AGED 26 - - - - 2013

I can't say how many times I've been seated here in the front row of the Gilfillan Auditorium listening to a guest speaker; or how many times I've stayed afterwards until the room is completely empty to review my notes, but anything for Brando. Soon enough I'll again be amidst the empty plastic chairs which are welded in lines along the ascending rows which make diagonal stripes of black and orange - OSU school colors diagonally running from the back wall to the front. Now though, as we have a new guest speaker and another possibly pointless lecture, the seats are filled with several hundred students parked behind their Mac Book Pros.

At first impression our speaker, Dr. Jill Bolte Taylor, has the sprouting promise to curb my addiction to psychology. Her fifty year old nasally voice is cruel to my eardrums. Her hippy-like, long, straight, silvery-grey hair makes me think she's either smoked too much pot or she's been caught up in her research for far too many years or maybe a combination of both.

In her favor, she's an acclaimed Harvard professor and neuroscientist. She's also made an appearance on Oprah and at my beloved TED convention for writing

My Stroke of Insight - a book where she writes about experiencing a stroke and being aware of it and making supposed groundbreaking psychological discoveries during the whole strife.

"I started studying the brain because I have a brother who has a brain disorder". She's now got the full attention of my frontal lobe. "I needed to know what it was about my brother's schizophrenia that he couldn't connect to a common and shared reality, but instead is delusional." I find myself reluctantly beginning to empathize with this woman as she continues. - "In pursuit of an understanding, in the lab of the Harvard department of psychology, I've been essentially mapping the micro circuitry of the brain. My associates and I were asking, which cells are communicating with which cells, with which chemicals and in which quantities of those chemicals? What are the biological differences between the brains of individuals who would be diagnosed as normal control compared with those who would be diagnosed with schizophrenia, schizoaffective or bipolar disorder?"

Five minutes in, she clicks a remote control and an x-ray image of a human brain emerges from the slide projector onto the pull-down screen behind her. "Implausibly, one morning in 1996, I woke up to this pain behind my left eye only to find I had a brain disorder of my own. A blood vessel exploded in the left half of my brain." As she describes her stroke and what happened to the sensor-motor area of her brain, a young man sitting to my right slips me a piece of folded notebook paper.

I open it and read Chris Hall in cursive. *Who's Chris Hall?* I roll my eyes, chidingly deciding if I can take the bore out of him. *Did this guy really just hand me a note with his name on it?* He looks back with patient green eyes as if he's waiting for me to rate him - so arrogant. I do rate him. His looks could make a girl insecure. His natural blonde highlights shimmer against his layered chestnut hair. His symmetrical face, clean shaven with a dimpled chin and smooth lips widen even more as he satisfyingly smirks. He knows he's good, but this class isn't Hook-Up 101. I lean in close to him, smile seductively and whisper, "I'm not your Juliet."

Dr. Taylor clicks for a new slide, a diagram of an average human brain.

"If you look at a human brain, it is obvious that the two hemispheres are completely separate. The two hemispheres do communicate with each other through the Corpus Callosum which is made up of some three hundred million axonal fibers, but other than that the two cerebral cortices are completely separate."

She states that the two sides process information differently and that the right hemisphere is all about the present moment; that it thinks in pictures and learns kinesthetically through the movement of the body.

"Information in the form of energy streams in simultaneously through all of our sensatory system and then it explodes into this enormous collage of what this present moment feels like, smells like, tastes like, sounds like and looks like. We are energy beings connected to the energy all around us through the consciousness of our right hemisphere."

She describes the left as a very different place, that it thinks linearly and methodically and that it's all about the past and the future - "It is designed to take the enormous collage of the present moment and pick out details and it then categorizes those details and organizes all that information and associates it with everything in the past that we've ever learned and projects into the future all of our possibilities. It thinks in language - that ongoing brain chatter that connects someone and his or her internal world to the external world. It's the little voice that says I am."

She explains that's the part of the brain she lost and describes how her brain's ability to process information slipped away in the course of four hours - how on the morning of the hemorrhage, everything slowed way down, until she lost fluidity and her steps became rigid - "I could actually hear the dialogue inside of my body. I heard a little voice say, OK you muscles you got to contract and you muscles relax. Then I lost my balance and there I was propped up against my bathroom wall. I looked down at my arm and I realized I could no longer define the boundaries of my body. I couldn't define where I began and where I ended because the atoms and the molecules of my arm blended with the atoms and molecules of the wall and all I could detect was this energy, *energy*."

She describes how her brain chatter, which is usually a function of the left hemisphere of the brain, became totally silent.

"What about coffee?" Chris whispers. I shake my head, keeping my attention on the speaker.

"It was just like someone took a remote control and pushed the mute button," she says as she points her remote and pretends to mute the audience. "At first I found myself shocked to be inside a silent mind, but then I was immediately captivated by the magnificence and the energy that was all around me. Because I could no longer identify the boundaries of my body, I felt enormous and expansive. I felt at one with all the energy that was, and it was beautiful."

"Imagine what it would be like to be totally disconnected from your brain chatter that connects you to the external world. I was in this space and my job and any stress related to my job was gone. And I felt lighter than my body. And all of my relationships and any stressors in the external world, they were gone."

It's something I can only imagine, but it sounds like a slice of heaven.

"And I felt this sense of peacefulness. And imagine what it would feel like to lose 37 years of emotional baggage. I felt euphoria. But then my left hemisphere came online and said hey you've got to pay attention. You've got to get help. I tried to get up, but then I felt my right side go totally paralyzed. Then I realized, oh my Gosh I'm having a stroke. Then the next thing my brain says to me is wow this is so cool." She has the sense of humor of a computer geek, but the auditorium laughs with her.

"How many brain scientists have the opportunity to study their brain from the inside out? Dr. Taylor jokingly asks. "I managed to call to a colleague - to me it sounded like two golden retrievers on the phone; but he recognized that I needed help and he called emergency services."

"Well?" Chris lures.

"Well what?" I politely smile. This doctor is talking about the most unique, most interesting stuff and Chris is only minding me. He's almost competing against my attention for Brandon.

"Coffee," he mouths with his smooth lips. I wonder if he'll shut up if I kiss him.

The doctor continued, "In the ambulance going from one side of Boston to the other, I curled up into a ball and like the last bit of air leaving a deflating balloon, I felt my spirit surrender and leave my body. I felt expansive like a genie liberated from her bottle."

I sense students leaning forward in their seats.

"My spirit sailed free like a great whale gliding in a sea of silent Nirvana. I remember thinking there is no way I will be able to squeeze the enormousness of myself back into a tiny body. But then at some point during this experience I realized I was in the hospital bed and still alive. I was still alive and I'd found Nirvana. And then I realized if I'm still alive and if I've found Nirvana then everyone can find Nirvana."

"I pictured a world filled with beautiful, peaceful, compassionate, loving people who knew that they could come to this space anytime they wanted. And that they could purposely choose to step to the left or the right hemisphere and find this peace. What a tremendous gift this experience could be. What a stroke of insight this could be to how we live our lives. And it motivated me to recover," she said and I realize it's an awe moment for the auditorium. No wonder she was on Oprah.

"Two and a half weeks after the hemorrhage they went in and removed a blood clot the size of a golf ball," she says commenting on a slide of her that shows half of her head shaved and an upside down horseshoe cut sutured together with large stiches. "It took me eight years to completely recover, but when I finally did I was on this mission to tell humanity that we are brothers and sisters. We are the life force power of the universe with manual dexterity and two cognitive minds; and we have the power to choose moment by moment who and how we want to be in the world."

Dr. Taylor clicks the remote for another slide. An outlined diagram of the human body illustrating the location of most of the running nerves inside it appears on the screen. The image has small subtext off to the side labeling the Cranial nerves which go from the brain to the eyes, mouth, ears and other parts of the head. More subtext labels the peripheral nerves which go from the spinal cord to the limbs, heart, lungs, stomach, intestines, and bladder and sex organs. "Again, information in the form of energy streams through our sensory system and into the brain."

Dr. Taylor calls on someone who must have raised a hand. "What do you mean by information?"

She answers, "That's a good question. Information usually starts out as experience from one or all of the five senses. Using language, the brain then converts the information into thoughts. If you break the thoughts down further, the root is energy. Now for me, this point brings us from psychology to sociology, especially since I've been on my mission." She pauses as students murmur and the room tries to figure out what she means.

"Can anyone guess what the difference might be if those thoughts, which again are energy at the core, become negative as opposed to positive?"

"It changes our emotional state," someone guesses.

"Yes, collectively," Dr. Taylor affirms. "Think hypochondriac. Think someone who worries so much, typically about an illness, that he or she nearly summons an illness or worsens one that already exists." Many students again murmur and fidget.

"Even more horrific, think blackout," Dr. Taylor says quieting the room. The fidgeting stops.

"Wait," someone says. "So are you standing behind the controversial notion that we brought last year's darkness upon ourselves?"

"Well I would be foolish to answer that because I don't know," Dr. Taylor answers. "I'm standing behind the notion that last year's marveled event or catastrophe or whatever you want to call it was nettled by our negativity. Surely you've heard the argument before that the world had met its demise with global warming, pollution, exhausted fossil fuels and natural resources, and not to mention the beginning of overpopulation. It's not an original theory, if anyone caught Bill O'Reilly's rant about it, or Barbara Walter's 20/20 special or Time magazine's numerous editorials. Do I have to go on, or have we heard this argument?"

"Sure, we know, yeah," the audience says together.

"Sorry, but what about eco-friendly efforts to help the planet; what about organizations like Greenpeace," someone else speaks up.

"Of course, there have always been positive influences, but maybe not enough. Regardless of the people making efforts to help, most of the population allowed the world to corrode and deteriorate." Dr. Taylor is met with a room full of wide-eyed, guilty faces. The topic makes me feel a little guilty too. I have to admit that I didn't do too much to help. Like most people, until the blackout, I took the world for granted. The Brandon puzzle was my excuse.

Avoiding a detour, Dr. Taylor stays on task. "The blackout is already history's most talked about topic. We could discuss theories all day. The point I'm getting at is that we are beings composed of energy, and last year we all experienced a depletion of energy."

Much of the room nods in agreement. Chris looks at me again.

"Good amino acids," Chris whispers, again promoting his coffee idea. Mildly humorous, his comment causes me to look over. Inside a grey zip-up hooded sweatshirt, draped against an athletic chest is a black shoelace necklace with a black, plastic whistle at the end.

"So, you're a jock, or a lifeguard or something?" He looks down at the whistle and then back up at me. "Swim team assistant coach," he whispers.

TRANSCENDENCE - - - - Brandon AGED 28 - - - - 2013

TRANSCENDENCE - - - - Brandon AGED 29 - - - - 2014

Eamesy, with as much focus as he can will himself to bring, bunts the soccer ball over the skipping rope, which is stretched tight and tied to the tops of two separate chairs. The soccer ball almost makes it to the ground, but I lunge to get my toes there just in time to juggle the ball once, twice. On the third go, I kick the ball with the side of my foot and it barely scrapes above the rope and back over to Eamesy's half of the mini court. The rope and chairs serve as our makeshift soccer-tennis court, here in the Miami Masters player lounge. Jake Eames, my new coach and hitting partner, plays this soccer-tennis game with me to help warm up my footwork before my match. It also helps my competitive mindset. I beat him 21 to 18. Then of course, I do a quick celebratory fist pump to seal the deal.

I'll be called to play my first match shortly. Time to grab a racket, and a ball. There's no time to waste. Time to practice my bounces.

First round is what I'm staring at straight ahead, and the first couple of rounds in a tournament are important because it's where commitment takes place. This is the most prestigious tournament I've ever played, so in my case, I'm committing to this caliber of tour level competition – top 100 ATP rankings. I'm only ranked 234 at the moment, but I did win my last three challenger events, Honolulu, Dallas, and Wolfsburg. I'm also the 22nd highest ranked American, and I'm rising. I'm a decade older than most up-and-comers, but the tournament director granted me entry into this tournament via a wildcard because he said, "Brandon is nowhere near retirement."

Now, for me to sink my teeth into this event, I need to feel good. I need to feel competitive. Fortunately, I do.

Racket.

Ball.

I dribble the ball with the racket in my right hand for about 500 bounces, and then switch hands to do the same thing with my left. I do mini upward bounces with the racket in both my right hand, and then my left. I alternate flip-flopping the racket to get the fore and backside of both of my hands to feel warmed-up. Bounce, bounce, bounce, bounce, bounce, bounce, bounce, bounce, bounce. I do bounces until my forearms burn. I do bounces until I can't feel my forearms burn. Jake and the rest of my coaching staff lightheartedly chat and joke amongst each other while I do about fifteen minutes of bounces. It gets my mind right. It always has. I do more bounces. Bounce, bounce, bounce, bounce, bounce, bounce, bounce. I see the ball better and better. I see anything that needs my focus better and better. My mind is like one of those hand crank flashlights. The more bounces, the longer I'll last. Bounce, bounce, bounce, bounce, stop.

Journal time. Time to rehearse my daily affirmation. It's quiet around the corner sofa over there, behind my team's chatter. That'll be the spot. I sift through my tennis bag in search of my journal before heading over.

My bag, which is at my feet and subject to my hands foraging around for the journal, is on the floor in the middle of the player lounge, which is temporarily furnished with couches and coffee tables, a pool table, a ping pong table, a poker table, arcade games, and a snack bar.

"Nole! what's happening man?" Bernard Tomic stands from his reclined group to greet Novak.

"Bernie! Good work last week. I watched your match versus Simon," Novak grins.

"I thought you were flying," Bernie responds. "WiFi on the plane?"

"Yeah, I watched it online."

"Yeah, well, glad you're back and ready to compete this week."

"Oh Haaa! OK another set of ping pong right now. I'm still up by four sets. And if you lose, you owe me another hundred dollars."

"Oh please, I just beat Janko in two sets, and I beat Kyrgios before that. I'm on fire." Bernie does a little fire dance.

"OK we'll see. I know where you break down."

"I don't break down, mate. I'm on fire."

The lounge is also actively occupied with pro players, their coaches, their friends or family, and tournament officials. Many players methodically go through their typical routines before being called out to play their matches. Dogopolov works the armbands with his coach. James watches match footage from yesterday on his iPad. Victor isn't meant to play for a while, but he's playing the role of KGB, shaking down a few other players at the poker table. Some of the young guns, like Thompson and Williams, bob their heads to headphones and laptops on the sofas near the snack bar. Rightfully so, no one is concerned when I sit by myself on the couch behind my team.

Both faces of my 6 by 9 inch, leather-bound journal press against the glass of the table as I write. I write what I always write. By now, I've written this passage so many times that I don't need to write it. It's tattooed onto my brain. But this daily monologue helps just like the bounces. So I write.

I write it and I speak it. I rap it. I chant it:

This could be my last moment on earth. I am grateful for my last moment.

I am grateful for an energy filled, physical environment, and a body and a mind to drive. This is my identity.

I am grateful for family and friends and supporters and spectators, everyone who brings energy to the moment.

I am grateful for my opponent. He gives me attention, and competes against me, causing me to keep alert. In my alertness, I am full of intention to play and win, to be my biggest self.

No matter how much my opponent tries, I play with more effort, and more wit, and more skill. I anticipate my opponent's shot. I react immediately. I move into position early. I hit the ball clean. I hit the most effective shot to easily win the point. I am more consistent and more accurate than my opponent. I outplace my opponent.

I am in control. I keep my opponent neutral, or on the defensive, until I hit a winner.

I am in flow state. I am a song bird's song. I am inspired. I inspire.

I write it again. I say it. I rap it. I chant it.

I write it again. I say it. I rap it. I chant it.

Louder and louder. More intense. More energy.

I write it again. I say it. I rap it. I chant it.

My team is next to me, but I barely hear them. There's commotion in the player lounge. More and more of it is focused on me. But I can barely tell what it's about. I'm zoning.

I write it again. I say it. I rap it. I chant it.

Then, I come to.

I'm alert, awake.

I must have caused a scene, and not realized it. My team, other players, and other people stare at me in wonderment. My team acts like they are about to consol me. Before they can, the tournament director pops his head in the entry.

"Brandon, you're on now."

I look around the room, but don't answer to anyone.

"Alright let's do it," I say. I turn to get a racket in hand out from my racket bag so I'm armed when I walk onto court. I grab the racket bag and my gear bag, sling them over my shoulders, and follow the tournament director.

Alex, my opponent, is already waiting with a tournament official in the entryway to stadium court. We're playing a center court match because we are both American citizens, and the USTA, United States Tennis Association wants to promote American tennis. Ironically, even though Alex has grown up in the States, he was born in Russia.

"OK, Brandon is here. We're ready," the tournament director speaks into his hand held radio.

"Brandon Christopher." My name is announced over surround sound stadium speakers. I'm being called out first, because out of Alex and me, I'm the lower ranked player. None-the-less, the enticing welcome applause puts a smile on my face as I walk out to court. Thousands of people I see. *How amazing that we'll all be focused on the same thing.*

"Alex Bogomolov Jr." The announcer gives his name a little bit more gusto, but it's no bother to me. I'm in love with this energy that is appearing. Fans cheer as Alex walks out. Even that makes me feel good.

We set our gear down, and jog to opposite sides of the net with our rackets in hand. The chair umpire there tosses a coin and points to Alex.

"Tails," Alex calls.

"Tails it is," the umpire proclaims after the coin lands on the back of his hand.

"I'll serve," he says.

"This side is fine," I say.

We both run back to our own baselines and start the ten minute warm-up, which I like to call the ten minute size-up. He's hitting clean on both sides, I notice as we hit ground strokes up and down the middle. *There's a tiny hitch with his left foot when he steps for a backhand, but it's not much to exploit.* His shots land deep in the court, inches from the baseline.

Just to give him a pop quiz, I pretend to shank a ball wide. He gets there with ease, and hits the ball back clean, just inches from the baseline. *This will be work, but that is what I expected.*

To "tree" in tennis means a player is playing better than himself, as if he suddenly grew several tree branches and can get a racket on anything. Play long enough or get into the zone mindset and days of treeing will come.

"Peaking" is when a player hits his physical peak and is playing the best tennis of his life - it's like treeing for two years straight. At thirty years old, Alex, currently ranked 25 in the world, is peaking.

As the match and long rallies get underway, he's no Federer, but his imposing force tracks down my erratic shot placement at what seems like the speed of sound as he consistently cracks forehands and backhands as loud as a rocket, and with the precision of a surgeon.

The 13,000 people in the stands "oooh" and "aaahh" as we spray balls within the lines, and sometimes out. Long rallies. Heavy hitting. A lot of winners. A few unforced errors.

We're both focused. We're both battling for the win. The crowd seems unbiased, but also seems to enjoy the level of performance. Their energies intensify as the match goes on. They're focused on what we're focused on. The attention fuels me.

Peaking Alex has been a pro long enough that hitting any sort of shot is second nature, so all he has to do is keep his eyes on the ball. That is, against most players, but I've been asking for more from him - more than the speed of sound, light-speed.

I'm serving 5-4, 40-30, for the first set. Beads of sweat drip from my forehead to the baseline as I dribble the ball with my left hand, getting ready for hopefully the final serve of the set. I dribble close to ten times. I take my time. The Key Biscayne humidity has a way of making a player feel like he's earned every point won, but the crowd sweats with me, so I feel like the workload is on all of us. Ace.

"First set, 6-4, Christopher," the chair umpire says over the mic.

Invigoration comes with the cheers.

During the changeover, I sit in my chair, under a towel, and try to relax. I can't. The crowd is too much invested, and there's more work to be done.

Alex makes advances during the second set, trying to push us to three, but I wipe him out in another 6-4 victory.

"Game, set, match," the chair umpire announces. "Christopher wins 6-4, 6-4."

"Come on," I celebrate as I spin and wave to the crowd. Jake, the rest of my coaching staff, mom and dad, Cassandra, and Amber, my girlfriend, are on their feet in my player box, smiling like kids at a birthday party. This win is their win too.

I trot over to them for hugs. They hug me tighter than expected. Group hug.

"OK I gotta go," I pry myself away. "Jake, I'll see you in the locker room."

"Remember, you have to do press after you change," Jake says.

My fête reached the press room before I do. There are many different reporters from different sources.

"There are rumors that your preparation just before the match was unorthodox. Can you tell us about that?"

"Is that a regular occurrence?"

"How long have you been playing tennis?"

"Where do you train?"

"What are your goals?"

"How long do you plan to compete on tour?"

"What influence do your parents have on you?"

It's a frenzy, but it's fun. The player party held at LIV night club in Miami is a similar scene. From the moment our crew unloads from two SUV's, all the way to the door we are spotlighted, delivered ahead of paparazzi, fans, and people in lines who wait to get in. We get mobbed with questions, my parents as much as me. It's an abridged press conference.

"Is there another planned mission trip?" "How long has your son been playing tennis?" "Brandon, how long have you been playing tennis?"

"Brandon, are you doing it for the people?" a reporter shouts. "Do you plan to be the people's champ?"

I smile, luring in the reporter, "Did you see what I did to Alex on court?"

"Yeah," he says.

"Well, you're next."

"You're coming for me," he laughs, confused.

"I'm coming for everyone!"

Other reporters have tuned in.

"How can you compete against everyone?" The reporter grabs onto a sliver of a moment that allows him to be a real Costello.

"I'm coming for everyone and you're first!"

Inside of the club is like an Omnimax theatre. A curved ceiling umbrellas everyone in the joint. It glows in a dark blue with lilac specks.

Subtle pink lights accentuate running staircases and white, leather lounge furniture. Out of reflex, my attention is drawn to other tennis players in the club: Maria Sharapova, Thomas Berdych, Ryan Harrison, Carolyn Wozniacki, Richard Gasquet. Two of the Frenchmen, Jo-Wilfred Tsonga and Gael Monfis, get down with a few girls over by the DJ booth. Former WTA player, Anna Kournikova and her Enrique mingle in the VIP section with basketball stars, Dwayne Wade and LeBron James.

"You've certainly met some ambitious demands," Dad shouts over the music, reaching for a glass of champagne. For Mom and Dad to get to my match, it was perfect timing.

"Yeah well, I'm not the one going into outer space." In the past eight weeks, Mom and Dad completed astronaut training in the Caribbean. Their next mission is a Virgin Galactic adventure.

"Oh it'll be more common than you know before you know it."

"Well maybe," I laugh. "But either way, thanks for coming to see me before you leave. And thanks for coming out tonight."

"Absolutely," Mom says. "We would obviously stay longer if we could."

"I was willing to pull an all-nighter and get my catch-up sleep on the shuttle," Dad jokes.

"Not happening, honey."

"I'm not sure which one of you has my best interest at heart. One of you wants to keep me up partying all night while the other is trying to get me lost in space," Dad pretends to be flustered.

"So are you guys ever going to settle down?"

"You're older than us. You go first." Dad says.

"Yeah right, I'm not retiring any time soon."

"Well then, why should we?"

"Haha I don't know. By the way, I'm starting a network," I tell them. "It's called Sideways-8."

"Sideways-8," Mom repeats. "Like Infiniti."

"Sounds ambitious," Dad says.

TRANSCENDENCE - - - - Brandon AGED 45 - - - - 2030

The digital clock reads: 2030, April 9th, 11:59:30 Pacific Standard.

The Canon building just off of Oak Street, downtown Portland, isn't one of the taller buildings in a city of ever increasing skyscrapers accommodating the three million plus and growing residents, but it's one of the most centrally located. The rooftop is a highly visible stage to the surrounding buildings - and to the people in those buildings; it's like box seating at the theatre.

In a grid of city blocks, to promote and uphold forestation, zoning regulations require that thirty percent of the blocks be maintained as public parks while the other seventy percent are skyscrapers. However, persuaded by political peer pressure, most of the building owners grow lush gardens on the roofs. The gardens are bordered by thin solar panels running along the top edges of each building. The Canon building is designed in similar fashion, only in the middle of the garden there is a circular courtyard, twenty five feet in diameter.

On opposite ends of that courtyard, two bodies, each wearing red, silk pajamas, lie faced down. Between them, in the very center of the roof, a young girl in a pink dress looks down at her pink high heels.

11:59:31 ...

"Nice suit," Brittany says coming in over the 60 inch monitor mounted on the kitchen wall of my downtown penthouse. "It looks good in the lighting. We should have chosen black lights."

11:59:32 ...

"Yeah, cool blue, is that your birthday suit," Allison playfully asks, coming in over a different screen on the same monitor.

11:59:33 …

Walking around the granite-topped kitchen island toward the balcony, "I'm glad my couture impresses," I play back referring to my ivory colored suit now doused in blue lighting. "So are the numbers still increasing?"

11:59:35 …

"By the second," Allison says, also flooded in blue.

"Yeah, same here," Fabian says coming in over another screen on the monitor, another blue face.

11:59:36 …

Just inside the opened sliding glass door, I gaze out over the Canon building to check out all who see. "Guys, I'm looking at thousands of blue rooms here," I speak up, excited.

11:59:39 …

"I'm looking at the same thing," Fabian says.

11:59:40 …

"Yep, same" - Brittany - Delhi

"Tons" - Allison - Seoul

"Thousands" - Fabian - Mumbai

"Yeah" - Tim - Sydney

"Heaps" - Ryan - London

"Thousands" - Keiko - Tokyo

"Yeah tons" - Blake - Mexico City

"Same" - Jonathan - New York City

"Same" - Jasmine - Sao Paulo

"Yeah thousands" - Sonny - Moscow

"It's hectic" - Asky - Shanghai

"So many" - Mona - Cairo

"Unbelievable" - Katie - Tehran

11:59:42 …

Though we are each in different cities, we are looking out at the same scene. "Worldwide baby," I shout. My excitement seemingly shared by the others, and hopefully shared by everyone in the other rooms and other buildings giving attention to the central rooftop stage.

11:59:55 …

After a moment of anticipation, "Are we ready?" Jonathan says.

11:59:56 …

"Three"

11:59:57 …

"Two"

11:59:58 ...

"One"

11:59:59 ...

"Happy Birthday Brando," everyone says collectively, coming in over the monitor.

Noon ...

Base thumps through the speakers of everyone who has the blue lighting turned on. Music starts. It drums kick, kick, clap... kick, kick, clap... kick, kick, clap... The two bodies lying faced down on the roof of the Canon building come to life, rise to their feet, and spin into acrobatic dance moves, accentuated by the beat. Synchronized with each other and synchronized with the other acrobatic duos on the other rooftops of the other designated cities, they twirl and then bound into the air to turn aerial cartwheels. At their midair peak, another layer of music joins the drums, to Bach's cello Suite No. 1.

Also midair, bright purple digital ink shoots out of both hands of one of the dancers like ink from a squid. At the same time, bright yellow digital ink shoots from the hands of the other dancer. A discrete contraption on their wrists allows for the Spiderman-like skill, the paint-trail reaches a curvy ten feet in length. It nearly floats following every move of the dancers' hands like elongated streamers. Dancing around the girl in pink, they create calligraphic designs in the air, swirls, curlicues, corkscrews. A third layer joins the music - a bamboo flute.

It's an amazing birthday present, but I hope it's a present for all those who watch. Blue windows continue to light, one after another, which makes me feel like I manifested the thought. Blimp cameras fly overhead to transmit the performance to global news syndicates. The symphony pulses through our speakers in such an attention grabbing manner that if it were placed as background music to anyone's daily life, anyone at all, the footage would win an Oscar. However, combined with the scene of the busy city currently being painted by purple and yellow digital streamers, surrounded by a garden of lush greenery, surrounded by tall buildings of thousands of blue lit rooms and windows, it's like watching Monet at work - mesmeric.

Then with no introduction, the girl in pink starts to sing, her head still down, she looks at her feet and takes steps as lightly as possible as if not to leave any footprints. She starts softly.

My face in the mirror - unfamiliar

I try to relate, but I don't even know

Her face is young and wrinkle free as is the faces of the other young protégés whom accompany her from the other cities. To ensure this is not a solo act, their combined vocals reverberate through the speakers of my penthouse and everyone else's apartment or office who have the blue lights turned on, indicating that they are listening.

This moment being shared worldwide, wouldn't have been as easy in the olden days, but with automatic, electronic translators, people communicate in 'Spanglish' to the tenth power, parts of every nation's dialect forming a universal language. En masse, the nouveau performance continues without missing a beat.

Their voices united are still soft and angelic. The young girl in the pink dress looks up at the people in the blue rooms and acts as though she's confessing a secret, her prowess engaging.

> **To try to make things clearer**
>
> **There's a question I tend to pose**

Passion grows as the global choir gets louder, singing a distinct R & B melody for the chorus.

> **Tell me more about yourself**
>
> **I'm into it, I want to know**
>
> **Maybe we share a common thread**
>
> **A single strand, you never know**

The dancers continue to seduce the audience with waves and flares of their digital streamers.

> **Tell me more about yourself**
>
> **I'm into it, I want to know**

> Maybe we share a common thread
>
> A single strand, you never know

I'm hoping the message behind this song rings true for those listening - that we are our perspectives…

> But never a reply, no reply, no reply
>
> So then I look at what I have inside
>
> Finding something awry
>
> So unbearable that I have to step outside

And also that we can live harmoniously despite our human qualities…

> Then I step outside myself
>
> And it's like I realign myself
>
> When I step outside myself
>
> I see the world and all its wealth
>
> When I step outside myself
>
> It's like I realign myself
>
> When I step outside myself
>
> I see the world and all its wealth

The dancers continue to add digital paint to the lyrical canvas…

> A transformation where I shine so bright
>
> My sights set from the ocean to the sky
>
> I'm like a star that shines at night

I'm a star shining in the day

The digital ink brightly shines here during midday just as it brightly shines in the cities where it is nighttime. And the global choir shows the most gusto yet, each singer really pushing their powerful pipes to the max...

I am the light

The singers reach pitch perfect form, hitting higher notes...

I am the light

Matching the triumphant, vocal dynamite, the dancers display a whirlwind of high-energy...

I am the light

Then the acrobatic dancers run together, past the courtyard's edge, through the garden and off the building. Their silk outfits reveal flying squirrel-like wings as the dancers glide down to the street below - a graceful exit. The girl in pink takes a bow receiving a thunderous applause from the blue rooms. It's something we are all a part of, worldwide. A brief performance, but a perfect representation of what we've worked so hard to build, the Sideways-8 Network...

TRANSCENDENCE - - - - Brandon AGED 49 - - - - 2034

Mom sits next to Dad as she writes the last bit of a church devotion. She's forged ahead with her loyal editorials every week, even on top of the unyielding work that goes into their HowYaTraveling organization.

Her brow furrows as she concentrates on her written words,"-for that brief moment, there were no Asians, no Europeans, and no Americans. For that moment, we were purely God's children, united by a love that crosses all barriers, brought to the light by the talent of one worn out old man who appeared to have been long ago rejected."

Still as religious as ever, it's her passion that has her always switched on. After all, even though technology advances by the nanosecond, until teleportation becomes a common transport, what better to do on a flight than exercise her influential voice? They're on the way to India, another mission.

"It's not just cultural; it's all of humanity. I'm just saying the population is going to be nine billion in less than a decade," Dad responds to Peri across the aisle. About to follow up, his speech is interrupted by strong turbulence.

The pilot interjects over the intercom, "We're coming into an electrical storm here so let's all stay seated and fasten our seatbelts."

Dad's shoulder bumps into Mom's as they buckle up. Turbulence keeps shaking the plane. The door of the cockpit swings open, and loudly uttering is a beeping only muffled by increased engine noise as if the pilot tries to accelerate us out of the storm.

There's a vivid flash of lightning and an explosion as the left engine ignites in flames. The plane smokes. The oxygen masks fall from their compartments. "We lost an engine, hang on."

The plane tailspins, it's dizzy and disorienting. "Honey," Dad says.

"I love you," her reply. "Forgive us, Lord, for our sins," she says faithfully repenting, her hand to Dad's. "We open our hearts to you."

"I love you honey," Dad says, trying to seize stability. The bullying G forces gang up on them.

A two minute terrifying, trembling free fall, "Brandon, Brandon, I know you can hear me," Mom beckons me. Her voice is distant; the beeping from the cockpit suddenly grows louder. "Heroism is love -

The sound of the phone beeping takes me away from the nightmare and back to reality. Squinting, the caller ID indicates that it's Chelsea.

"Answer," I command as Chelsea appears in hologram form over the visual display module above the dresser in my bedroom. What was Mom saying, I wonder, but then notice tears running down Chelsea's face. I'm wide awake. "What's wrong?" I say reaching for a robe.

"It's Mom and Dad," she exhales.

"What happened?" Fully awake, a chill runs down my spine and not because cool air drifts in through the cracked window, but because Mom's words linger. *What was she getting at?*

Chelsea blubbers out the news in between her tears, "A crash, their plane went down over Bangladesh, no survivors."

A fleet of five 767's full of people joining the mission, each plane scheduled to land in Mumbai twenty minutes apart. After each plane lands and unloads, travelers were meant to wait for the remaining planes, hosting a joyous assemblage greeting. It's a ceremony Mom and Dad have carried out since the beginning, relying on sheer numbers, the sum of all those involved, to raise spirits before the mission. This time instead of jubilation, the second through fifth plane were greeted with a story of great tragedy.

I start mentally compiling a list of my own - mentor, nurturer, disciplinarian, cheerleader, guide – what my parents were to me and many others.

"I just got off the phone with Kim. I told her I'd handle logistics and funeral arrangements. I can't believe I had the strength to do that. I can't believe this is real," Chelsea goes on unfazed by my silence. "They became these worldly icons. I guess I thought they were invincible. All they did was care for other people. They can't die. They *can't* die. They're heroes." She makes the dream real again. For an instant I'm in the trembling free fall of the plane, listening to Mom beckon me, *heroism is love.*

Well, being supportive to baby sis is at least a start. "You know Chels, they would say the same about you," I tell her, my eyes watering, realizing that I must now refer to Mom and Dad in the past tense. The hologram deceiving, I wish I could give her a hug and tell her everything's going to be alright. "You're just as important to the world you know."

After sliding on my Apple Inculade Ring, her holographic image follows me to the kitchen. "But I already miss them," she says racked by new sobs.

Her emotional state becomes irrational, "Don't *you?* Or are you going straight into some machine mode?"

"No, of course not," I respond, opening the tea drawer. "I'm not bypassing my feelings. I'm going to miss them terribly. If anything I'm thinking about their love and I can feel it. I'll tell you something. Mom talked to me in my sleep."

"From heaven," Chelsea asks, holding back another current of tears, believing that with me anything could be possible.

"No, I think just before the crash," I say. "But do you know how much they selflessly loved us?"

"Yeah," she answers.

"They tried to share that love with the world."

"I know," she says.

"Well that was them, always. That was their gift of reverence. And the world will certainly be at a loss without them, but we can keep them alive by spreading that reverence, by treating the world as our family. And you have that in you, the way you looked out for me before I was really awake, the way you look out for your family now. We have to be strong so the world is not at a loss. Do it for Mom and Dad. Do it for your twins."

"What should we do?"

"We can talk about that, but first let's meet up. How are Chris, and the kids?"

TRANSCENDENCE - - - - Brandon AGED 65 - - - - 2050

My view out the spaceship window is of our most faithful commune, which is currently settled into the public viewing gallery, doing what they do best. For the time being, they're making the viewing gallery their home as they wait for our launch. As is their nature, everywhere they go, they respectfully yet commandingly act as if they own the space they occupy. It's part of owning the moment.

Since the Blackout, and since the world has reformed, the Avante-Gardes have formed subcultures around the world just as bodacious as the hippies of the 1960's. And though that was nearly a century ago, the freethinking, bohemian attitude is just as prevalent among today's A.G.'s or 'Agies'. But unlike the hippies, they *age* gracefully into contemporary times the way lifelong actors do. And as progressive mavericks they continue to learn, invent, and be on the forefront of the future.

Most importantly, we spearhead any and all potential roadblocks which may hinder the quality of life in the future. That's what this extraterrestrial mission to planet Udry is all about - more room for more people. Originally known as planet Gliese 581 d from the Libra constellation, the planet was discovered in 2007 by Swiss astronomer Stephane Udry.

"One minute until countdown," Julie says. Though the six of us on board are now fully trained and certified astronauts, she is the only one of us who has been training since she was a child. As an astronomer, astronaut, fellow Avante-Garde, and daughter of Stephane Udry, Julie is leading our mission to help us prove if the planet orbiting the red dwarf star is indeed habitable.

Still looking out the circular window, my gaze wanders across two acres of Richard Branson's Spaceport simply consisting of the terminal hangar and other space planes on other runways. Then onto a tiny town in the neighboring five acres, mostly hotels and restaurants, all surrounded by New Mexico desert. It's the same view my parents shared before they launched into space, thirty seven years ago when space travel became common.

Looking over the land makes me think, *the land, is it undeveloped or is it preserved?* It's a mutual thought and never successfully answered by any of mankind, a debate that's caused political controversy, sometimes to the dire extremes of war. And who's suited to answer? As Branson was making his mark here, many archeological sites were uncovered from thousands of years ago finding ancient tools and pieces of pottery, which are on display inside the Spaceport museum. Beneath one of the artifacts, some sort of hammer, is an engraved label with a quote from Branson. "Upon the surface of the future, one is busy with archeology." More surface is why we push the envelope, seeking alternative living.

"Now's the time for final goodbyes," I tell the guys. "We'll be back in forty thousand light-years." Strapped into our reclining seats, we wave our goodbyes, a little nervous through the small windows as if we are embarking with kayak to ocean - twenty thousand light years of outer space each way - *talk about traveling across the abyss.*

"10…9…," mission control comes through our headsets. Just seconds away from creating a future home for the Jetsons. For an instant, the countdown has me back in my old penthouse in Portland, listening to the worldwide rooftop choir. Hearing the countdown in the background, I surf my mind's memories.

"…8…7…," mission control is the theme song, Sideways-8's undertakings are the ambiance. I remember Japan, giving hope to the power of wishes when we gave flight to one million folded paper cranes, a wish for every thousand.

"6…5…" I'm in Washington D.C., on the verge of WWIII, when Sideways-8, HowYaTraveling, Green Planet, the Illuminati, Microsoft, Apple, Canon, and hundreds of thousands of other charities and company nations marched as Avante-Gardes in the biggest peace faction in history.

"4…3…" I'm in my office making love to my work, giving inception to accomplishment, always heading for the dawning of potentiality. Sideways-8, my organization designed to be in a permanent merging phase; from spiritual retreats to spiritual missions to spiritual centers; from talent mentorships to talent representation to talent production; from community service to global resources research.

Hopefully my greatest impact has been on what's to come… that or maybe it will be my commitment to the arts, encouraging everyone to live as an artist. I believe perception is life. I believe perception is an art, how we see and how we act. The process of simply existing is art. I include myself in that ideal, my journey.

Flashing before my eyes, I recall my existence within Zosimos, Kul, Wolf, Lion…

"…2…1," signaling the commencement to yet another pivotal moment. The engine rumbles and the hydrogen accelerators fire. Like the kick of a bazooka, I feel a heave as we take off. Our speed increases. We'll be flying as fast as the speed of light when we breach the Ozone layer.

TRANSCENDENCE - - - - Chelsea AGED 63 - - - - 2050

The sound of Brandon tugging at his seat belt has me turn my head. My peripheral vision barely reaches him. "Brandon," I query, glancing at the journal that rests on his lap. I've still yet to look in there.

He doesn't respond, just continues working his seatbelt. It's as if he's conducting a safety check, pulling at the buckle, testing its tight hold.

He suddenly stops testing the belt. His head, which droops over his left shoulder, rolls upright as his eyes trail to mine. Coercing a response, "Brandon," I nod as his eyes seem to readjust on me. Then, quickly, his eyes glaze over and his head rolls to the right as he mutters "forty thousand….light..." *What did you say? He's gone again. It's been sixty years of this bullshit.*

Emotions about to betray me, "Brandon, do you know where we are going?" I ask as gently as possible.

No response. "Mom, Dad, what do I do?" I pray.

"Brandon, we are going to meet with Dr. Durig," I say persisting. If nothing else, I'm humoring myself. Brandon's hand reaches up, motioning me to stop. Actually, it's more like he's waving at me. Then, from peering out the window, he looks at me again. This time it's with bold eye contact. The new staring contest makes me feel as though he's reading my mind. It takes me a little by surprise. A tear escapes and trickles down my cheek. "Do you see me?" I implore.

His lips move subtly, about to say something. Then his eyes glaze over, again, and his head rolls back as he looks up at the car ceiling. Unable to help myself, I try again, to stir his awareness. "Brandon, Dr. Durig has outstanding credentials. He's -

I turn away, looking forward. I can sense David, our escort, whom I'm sitting shotgun next to - his mannerisms toiling with hesitation. He's questioning himself - whether or not to console me. But he knows better. This isn't the first time he's seen me flustered over Brandon issues. Truth be told, I *could* go for some consoling.

I can't keep from crying now. "I love you Brandon," I bewail to myself. "This is too much!"

Then, suddenly, another sound comes from the backseat - shrieking gasps. Out of my peripheral vision, again, I see Brandon struggle. He grabs at his chest with his right hand as if he's having a heart attack. "Brandon!" I scream.

I could just as easily swivel my seat back to face Brandon, but the panicked child in me unleashes urgent helplessness. I unbuckle and try to climb over, my knee ramming the center shifter in the process -

I'm unexpectedly whiplashed in-between the front seats - consequence of the car swerving. It quickly dawns on me, what I must have done - when I bumped the shifter with my knee, I must have switched it off autopilot.

David now hastily trying to prevent…

TRANSCENDENCE - - - - Brandon AGED 65- - - - 2050

At 6'11, Thomas "High Top" Jenkins was taller than anyone he knew. When he was still growing, his father told him to play basketball. "Pay for the family." At age 18, his full grown size and overbearing force earned a scholarship to UCLA. But, off court, his overdue, unrestrained force, fatal to his father and his father's abusiveness, instead, paid for three hots and a cot at California's iron-barred motel.

On his 21st birthday, High Top was released early. It was his good behavior that put him in a halfway-house just outside of West Hollywood. Ironically, his parole officer assigned him to work custodial duties at a hospital at UCLA. Since then, his mandatory uniform has changed from an orange jumpsuit to a navy jumpsuit, but the chill that sometimes sneaks inside the fabric at 4:30 in the morning, the start of his shift, feels just as uncomfortable as it had for the previous three years of wearing a jumpsuit. The chill, that he knows must be owed to him, regardless of the undershirt, keeps him feeling bare, uncivilized.

On this May 1st, there's something particularly chilling about the L.A. air. After slipping in through the electronic doors at the Neuropsychiatric Hospital at UCLA, a hint of the chill hugs High Top, holding him tight for the elevator ride up. "Ding." An open door is the best feeling in the world. The fourth floor is dedicated to patients with Borderline Personality Disorder, and it's also where his janitor closet happens to be. Ready to work, he shakes off a shiver, very much in the mood for a hot cup of coffee. "Caffeine," he craves as he passes a watchful nurse who sits behind the reception desk. Authority – She's a reminder of his surroundings. He's still a captive here – to the quality of his conduct just as much as a job well done.

Recent memory strikes him – authority. It was ordered that he'd stay locked away in a guarded cell behind guarded walls, behind stiff tax payers' regulations. Society wanted him in there, caged with the other wild animals. The Good Book that made rounds on the inside declared equality among all humanity, but even as a growing boy, High Top was pressured to shrink in the corner of his bedroom away from the old man. "Would it ever be his time to live?" That thought constantly nagged him.

Only his mind navigated him through prison's timeline, and how fortunate he now feels because in here, all these patients are prisoners of their own minds. To avoid waking any of the patients, High Top quietly loafs down the hallway toward the kitchen. Passing the community lounge room along the way, he notices the back of Brandon's grey haired head overlapping the top of a recliner. *Maybe he's in the mood for another talk.*

The lounge is expansive, liberally open to anyone who wants to be a part of a well-mannered community. Protective, paneled windows along the back wall. The sky outside lightens. It subtly exposes the layout: coffee tables and sofas spread across a burgundy, carpeted floor. The style of the room is similar to that of a hotel lobby – the furnishings are homey yet impersonal – no individual's distinctions, except for whoever made the spew stain in the corner. High Top steps into the room softly, an excited, gentle gait, thrilled that Brandon might be awake. From their last few talks, he already sees Brandon as a fatherly figure. *For someone who lives in a mental hospital, he sure is a wise, old man.*

Just hours earlier, Brandon sits in the same recliner, watching the news. An anchorwoman reports updates about another globalization. Since the crash, and since Chelsea's death, he's vivified. *My sights are now on current world reality, but the reality I see is a world of deception – men living like robots.*

The digital pixels hover steadily. No light passes through the holographic image. "After this latest merger, the Canon network will employ 41 million people, bumping them a spot higher on the official Token Index," the anchorwoman reports behind a put-on smile. She doesn't really know the story. Some stories are sad. Some neutral. Some positive. She mirrors society's treatment towards her. She puts-on the way her bosses see fit.

As for her context of globalization, I can remember, as a child, when Ross Perot was running for U.S. president. He wanted to run the nation like a company. It is considered monumental that companies now run the world, and that governing nations are simply lenient mores. But, optimism in this notion is faith in a land of robots. The shifting of powerhouses is merely the appearance of progress, the supposed eminence of capitalism. The powerhouse is lust. If *only my earthly brothers and sisters knew their true identity*.

"Scientists have breached new stem cell discoveries relating to the brain," the anchorwoman reports, transitioning to a different story. I see it common the capability to clone and reproduce fresh, human organs. New limbs. New bodies. New brains. It's within us to develop super abilities, strengths and immunities. People want eternal invincibility. *But, again, if only they knew their true identity*.

We are in a world where most people fail to recognize that true eternal invincibility exists among the energy. Forty years ago, everyone was saved from this energy, yet most people don't tap into it as much as they could. Instead, they attach to their bodies. Attachment to material. It'd be nice to see people focus on being exactly who they are meant to be – full bloom.

Therein lays a potential utopia. Albeit a world of deception, the only thing needed is a realization of the beauty and preciousness about a fleeting, human journey. Then nothing will be ordinary, but extravagant. Baseness would fade. Discovery. Revelation. I sense this in due time. *Balance will prevail*.

"Shut down!" The hologram of the news disappears as it is programmed to recognize my verbal command. Sitting here, looking out the window, I have the ability to communicate with anyone – to help those who are lost. But, that's not my role. *After all, balance will prevail.*

My role was to live through induced visions – an insightful meditation, experiencing adventure, romance, and many scintillating varieties. The purpose was indirectly served, but it was served. It's now time for a different type of meditation.

Closing my eyes, I let go of such burdening concerns as fate. Watching thoughts go by: earth, humanity, love, hate, perfection, imperfection, perception, perspective, deception – I let go of them, lightening my mood.

I focus on: toes, feet, ankles, legs, knees, torso, chest, heart, lungs, shoulders, arms, neck, mouth, nose, eyes, ears, head, brain – I let go of it all, lightening.

I ponder truth – what it is that's real. Reality – is that what's physical? Physicality – Am I physical? I'm physically sitting in a chair, meditating. Is the chair real? I have no proof other than what my sensatory system indicates. I believe the chair is real. I *believed* the chair to be real. Was that bias? There is no chair. There is only my thought about the chair – my thoughts. Release the thoughts. I let go, lightening, lifting. Just be. Be. Be. Breathe. Air. Light. Lifting.

Hovering, floating, I find myself levitating.

Bright – brightness comes upon me.

Looking – I look down, and…

…it's my body.

My body is below – it's there, relaxed in the recliner. I'm out of body. I could go back, but…

…I consider death: euphoria, passivity, grandiosity, psychosis, catatonic. I consider life: free, inspired, devotion, visions, ecstasy, illumination. There's more life in an advanced state. I let go, relinquishing my body.

No more I – ONE. Absorption. Identity is action. BBBUUUUUZZZZZZ. Everywhere.

HHHHHHHHHHHHHHUUUUUUUUUUUUUU UMMMMMMMMMMMMM

Allness – it's energetic, exciting. It's easy to be.

HHHHHHHHHHHHHEEEEEEEEEEEEEEEEEEE EEEEEEEEEEEEEEEEEEE

Transcending into divinity.

Purity.

YYYYYEEEEEAAAAAAAAAUUUUUUUU WWWWWWWWWWAAAAA

High Top, approaching the recliner, comes around the front to find Brandon sleeping with a journal on his lap. Don't disturb him. He sleeps so peacefully. Peace has been High Top's biggest goal since he was a boy – personal peace – world peace.

Since meeting, there's always been an idealism about Brandon that High Top thoroughly admires.

Admiring Brandon's stature, High Top can see that idealism as if it's a giant aura. It has the mystery and strength of a genie. *He could probably grant miraculous wishes.*

Then, the chill, that earlier was early morning air, comes back, hugging High Top, making the hairs on the back of his neck stand. Double-take. Brandon is in such stillness that he appears lifeless.

High Top touches Brandon's cheek to find his skin cold. Stunned, High Top takes a step back. "He's gone…

…he's gone…

…but, did he leave?"

NAMASTE

TRANSCENDENCE - - - - Ari & Valentine AGED 6 & 7- - - - 2955

There's this buzzing energy in the ground. The birds and the both of us…

Made in the USA
San Bernardino, CA
18 November 2013